I0769483

AFTER glow

OTTAWA REGENTS, BOOK THREE

RUBY RANA

To those whose minds and bodies run wildly in opposite directions: you're not broken. Here's to turning the ache of your hopes and dreams into joy and success.

CONTENT/TRIGGER WARNINGS

This book contains mature themes and language, and is not intended for those under the age of 18.

While this is a romantic comedy, there are some serious themes such as childhood abandonment, social anxiety, internalized ableism and the ongoing struggles of being diagnosed with a learning disability and ADHD as an adult. There are also graphic depictions of sex, BDSM, and kink exploration between consenting adults.

If any of these topics are a trigger for you, please refrain from reading or proceed with caution.

PLAYLIST

Summersong - The Decemberists

I Wanna Be Yours - Arctic Monkeys

Hide Away - Daya

End of Beginning - Djo

Radio Gaga - Queen

Tujhe Yaad Na Mari Aayee - Manpreet Akhtar, Alka Yagnik, Udit Narayan

To Be Alone With You - Sufjan Stevens

Us - Regina Spektor

Mahiye Jinna Sohna - Darshan Raval, Lijo George

Love You Madly - Cake

Iris - The Goo Goo Dolls

Sleepyhead - Passion Pit

The Mountain is You - Chance Peña

Home - Good Neighbors

The District Sleeps Alone Tonight - The Postal Service

Carry You Home - Alex Warren

Belong Together - Mark Ambor

All I Want - Kodaline

Tu Meri - Vishal Dadlani

OTTAWA REGENTS ROSTER

Player Name	#	Position	Height	Weight	Birthday	Hometown
Fletcher Donovan	23	Center	6'3	207	Feb. 29	Summerside, PEI, CAN
Landon Radek	12	R Winger	6'2	190	Jan. 9	Mississauga, ON, CAN
Blake Szeczin	17	L Winger	5'8	175	Nov. 17	Chicago, IL, USA
Derrick Jaeger	10	Defenseman	6'6	233	Apr. 30	Truro, NS, CAN
Theron Olsen	28	Defenseman	6'4	228	Jan. 13	Saskatoon, SK, CAN
Wade Boehner	31	Goalie	6'4	210	July 28	Lac Ste. Anne, AB, CAN

CHAPTER 1:
I'M A LOSER

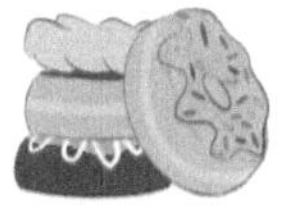

FLETCHER

February

MY COCK HAS ALWAYS BEEN AN ASSHOLE HELL-BENT on embarrassing me.

Being hard inside a double cup and soaking through the compression boxers isn't my idea of a good time, especially at the Ottawa Regents' annual family skate.

All because the goalie mentioned Behraz Irani in passing and then skated off for a photo shoot with his loved ones.

That's how it always starts. A small inkling, the most fleeting of ideas, sets off rich imagery from my memory of her dark eyes and even darker hair against fair, creamy skin, full, pink lips and rosy cheeks, the insane curves of her body, and ends with a wild series of fantasies.

We share the same social circle—the Regents' alternate captain, Landon, and my goalie, Wade, are married to her best friends—but I'm so far out of her orbit, I might as well be in another galaxy.

"Heads up!" A rogue puck whizzes by, and another forward, Blake Szeczin holds up a glove.

"Sorry!" I reply with a weak wave, watching my breath condensate over the ice as I look around.

Something about being in a space filled with people feels lonelier than when I'm on my own. Being one of seven kids growing up on Prince Edward Island left a hollow ache in my chest. The family has since doubled as my siblings got married and had kids, only exacerbating the feeling.

Signing with Ottawa was an easy escape but didn't heal the longing for companionship.

Now, don't get me wrong. The Regents are closer to me than my own family since I joined, but being surrounded by doting relationships is an especially painful reminder when you're perpetually single. If I sound jealous, it's because I am.

A few dozen feet from me is our long-standing captain, Derrick Jaeger. He poses with his wife, Skylar, kissing through a smile as Doug wags his tail and vies for attention between their skates with a *woof*.

Closer to center ice, the team's all-star, Landon Davé-Radek, turns his infant daughter to face the camera, bouncing her so the double poms of her toque wiggle like wheat in a breezy field. Indi pulls the two of them close, and Akhila's chubby cheeks spill past her tiny, round face when her parents lift her slightly and point to the embroidered #12 on her officially licensed, black and gold Ottawa Regents snowsuit.

Even our goalie, Wade, previously a well-known fuckboy, stands with Gabe Finch, the award-winning sideline reporter for the NHL. He looks at his new wife like Jaeger's dog looks at his humans.

Rightfully so. She's an incredible, gracious journalist, not to mention beautiful, though Wade would probably gouge my eyes out if I told him I thought his wife was pretty.

My eyes follow the gaggle of #23 jerseys skating behind the net, bumping and huffing between short races, taunting each other over missed goals, and taking silly pictures. Between my siblings, their spouses, and a handful of nieces and nephews, there are fourteen donning my name and number. Slightly fewer than usual, since Mom broke her foot and Dad stayed with her, and my youngest brother is somewhere in Croatia.

Fourteen family members, a full roster, and somehow, I still don't feel like I belong.

Another cloudy breath sighs from my nose.

Two of my sisters, Piper and Greer, round up their little ones and shepherd them out of the rink. Greer's eldest is having some sort of tantrum and lies down in rebellion. His dad attempts to appease him but loses patience and ends up hooking a hand into the footplate of his skate, preparing to drag him across the ice. Before they get far, Parker, my older brother, squats down and convinces him to stand.

It's much gentler than what I remember.

"Get up, Fletch."

I wiped away the threads of my snot with the back of my glove.

"And quit crying. You're not a baby anymore."

I was nine. He was fourteen. We were both babies.

My bloodied bottom lip quivered as I blinked back tears.

He tilted my head by the helmet roughly, taking a better look at the damage done by the opposing team's defenseman.

"It's a small cut," he said through a tsk. "Get it cleaned up and get back on the ice."

My cheek felt warm and heavy. "But it hurts."

"You don't even need stitches. I promise you're gonna deal with much worse. Now sit your ass on that bench so Coach Zeb can tape it."

A watery haze covers my vision momentarily, and when it clears, Parker catches my gaze.

His chin lifts in a sideways nod, but it isn't affirming. It's a directive.

I coast to him.

"Let's talk," he says flatly.

Suddenly, I'm fifteen again. Getting reprimanded for something likely out of my control.

"Quit being a little asshole and go after the puck!" Park yelled, slamming a fist on the boards behind the bench.

"That goon is way too big to be in the U16 league," I argued.

"Grow the fuck up, Fletcher. If I were you," —his jaw ticked, hand reaching for his bad knee— "you better convince your coach to let you play again. I swear to God, if you don't score a goal this period, I'll have you bag skating at the crack of dawn until you're sick."

We exit through the gap in the boards and slow to a stop in the hallway leading to the lockers. "What's up?"

"You extended your contract?"

My throat tightens. Who told him?

"Yeah."

Two fingers roughly massage his forehead as he exhales. "You couldn't negotiate any higher?"

I shrug. "It's only for a season."

He scoffs. "Didn't you win two Stanley Cups?"

"That was years ago."

"And whose fault is that?" His eyebrows rise in question. "I can't tell you how much it kills me to watch you throw this away. You've been on the team for nine years, Fletch."

"I know, but—"

"Nine *fucking* years. Is there a C on your sweater? An A? No? Are you a leading scorer, then?"

"I—"

"You could do so much better!" he grits through his teeth. Both of his hands stretch and curl into the space between us, as if trying to strangle air itself. "But no. Do you even care? Does it matter to you? That so many rely on you? Because for 750k, it sure as hell doesn't seem like it."

"Parker." Miller appears behind me, her hands akimbo. My almost-twin's telepathic connection is strong today.

My brother's not wrong, though. My stats have plateaued, if not steadily declined. I'm one of the lowest-paid in the league, and whatever I've earned for nearly a decade has gone mainly to the things my parents couldn't afford. Dad's gambling debts. Their mortgage. Covering housing, expenses, and tuition for my brothers and sisters while they were at university.

"You're being too hard on him." Mills stands between the two of us.

"He's wasting his potential. He could be so much more—"

As if I don't know that. Doesn't he think I want that? To play better? To earn respect amongst my peers in my profession? But I'm not like Landon or Wade. I don't have charm, wit, or skill. Hell, most times I can't even speak up. Ask me a question in a post-game interview or at a press conference, and I do my best to push away the anxiety and briefly answer. Tell me to inspire a locker room, or casually defend my life choices, and I'll hide in a washroom stall with only a toilet as a companion for all eternity.

But for some reason, this time, Parker's tone cracks me open.

I throw an arm up, effectively moving my sister to the side. "Maybe this is just how it is, Park. Not everyone is destined for greatness. I'm trying my best, and I'm doing okay."

I'm definitely *not* doing okay.

His skin reddens. "*This* is your best? You're so fucking aggravating. Do you even hear yourself?"

My sister cuts in again, her lips tightening into a line. "This is why he doesn't like coming home."

"Yeah?" Parker's green eyes bolt to mine. "Then don't come home."

The muscle in his jaw ripples before he turns to stomp away. As best as one can stomp away on a rubber floor.

Miller circles an arm around my padded waist and breathes out. "Sorry, he's such a dick, Fletch."

I reciprocate by squeezing her shoulder. "Don't worry about it."

My sister pulls her phone from a pocket with a half-laugh. "I'm gonna go help Cam. Rav fell asleep on his shoulder before he could get his skates off, and he's stranded."

"No worries," I say, worrying about literally every goddamn thing. "Call me when you get to the hotel."

Her tall frame disappears down the corridor in the opposite direction. I head to the locker room, hoping for some quiet time to sit with my guilt.

People say my brother's looking out for me, but Parker wants for me what he actually wants for himself. Sometimes it's like I'm living someone else's life. Playing puck and on the road all the time. I'd rather be in bed with a book, forgetting the world exists while sifting through well-worn pages. Bonus points if it's a comfort reread, and the Decemberists anguish softly in the background while sandalwood incense releases swirls of smoke around the room.

I can almost smell it, but the stench of hockey gear overpowers my imagination. My ass plops onto a bench.

"When they said family skate, I don't think they meant your *whole* family, Donny."

Goalies are notoriously weird *and* annoying, but Wade Boehner likes to remind us that he's not half as annoying as he once was, and nowhere near as annoying as he could be.

"A little late to be testing out a new nickname, dontcha think?"

"Fletchy doesn't have the same ring to it. Donny, on the other hand," —he snaps and points a finger gun at me— "Donny is solid. Shortened last names are classic."

I stand to remove the hockey sweater from my chest. "If you say so."

Landon does the same, just past Wade. "Why are you so mopey today? Is your brother still being an asshole?"

My left shoulder lifts and drops. "When is he not?" The bench welcomes my sweaty, padded ass again as I pry gear from my torso.

Wade gets rid of his chest protector and compression shirt, revealing a vintage-style heart tattoo on his left pec. In a blocky sports font, it reads *Property of Freckles.*

Lucky, loved-on bastard.

"Take a picture and sell it online, Donny," Wade interrupts my staring, "It'll last forever."

I roll my eyes.

"You, too" —his arms stretch apart — "could be property of a certain raven-haired beauty. If you weren't a big ol' scaredy-cat."

"I'm not a scaredy-cat."

I'm totally a scaredy-cat. The biggest.

"It's true, Fletch," Landon adds. At least he's not going along with Wade's new-nickname bullshit. "You've talked a big game over the years."

"Right? Remember that time he said he was gonna—" Wade clicks his tongue with a loud pop while thrusting his hips and miming seating someone on his lap. "*Whoosh.*" His hand moves mid-air as if swinging a revolving door.

I groan and hide my eyes behind clammy palms.

After several years, they can't let it go. I shouldn't be held responsible for something I said when my spongy, underdeveloped frontal lobe was soaked in scotch.

"I'd sit her on my cock and spin her like a top," were my exact words. The sentiment was as true then as it is now, but with no plan of execution, saying it out loud meant a lifetime of shit doled out by the starting lineup of the Ottawa Regents.

"You could make it happen, Donny." Wade claps a hand on my back. "We've been trying to introduce you two properly for years."

Believe me, buddy, it isn't for lack of trying. Any time I breathe the same air as her, I seize up like Jell-O in a bundt pan. I can't get a single word out. My brain short-circuits. Blood rushes to the surface of every inch of my skin in an offensive blush. And don't get me started on my face. I think about acknowledging her with a smile, but fear it appears as something else entirely. A leer, a sneer? Disgust? What if she takes it the wrong way? What if she thinks I'm stroking out?

What if I'm a loser?

Who am I kidding? I *am* a loser.

Behraz is a perfect, joyous goddess with a blindingly beautiful smile and a laugh that is nothing short of sunshine on a clear day. And unsurprisingly, for a pale ginger like me, it burns. Too long in her presence and I'll be cooked like a deep-sea lobster.

She's a social butterfly. I'm practically a pariah.

Wade's voice reaches my ears once more.

"...And, like, what's the worst that could happen? Bea's already *super* into you."

Yeah, right.

I reject the possibility. "You think *everyone* is *super* into *everyone*. She doesn't know I exist."

"*Uh*, yeah, she does. She used to come to games with your jersey on."

Oh, I remember. It had me bricked up during multiple games and drove me fucking insane.

"That doesn't mean anything. Maybe she got it on sale or something."

Why else would anyone want a loser's jersey?

Landon coughs out a laugh. "On...sale?"

"Hate to break it to ya, Donny, but you're an idiot." Wade runs a hand through his sweaty hair. "I mean, listen, you could continue as you have been."

"It's not so bad," I lie.

"Or you could quit hiding in books and fictional worlds all the time and start living out the life you dream about."

He's right, of course, but reality sucks. Reality is my social anxiety being so bad I don't have any friends except for these guys. Reality is my career taking a nosedive, and I have no idea what to do about it. Reality is—well, *shit*.

"I'm all for escapism, okay? This world is too fucked up not to want to. But don't do it because you're afraid." Wade toys with his wedding ring, revealing Hindi script inked underneath. He catches me staring again. "It says Gargi, Gabe's birth name."

Damn. The woman owns him in every way.

What I would do to belong to someone like that.

Landon picks up his phone and continues to undress. "Hi, baby. You're on speaker."

A coo echoes behind Indi's voice. "*You almost done?*"

"Not even close. I need to shower."

"Well, hurry up, Princess. I've gotta get Akhila to sleep in the car seat on the way to Bea's."

The three of us exchange surprised glances.

"We're going to Bea's?"

"Yeah, we promised to help her move."

"We did?" Landon's face cringes in Wade's direction. He exaggeratedly mouths, *Did you know about this?*

Wade shakes his head with a frown.

"She's moving again?"

Again?

My ears perk.

Indi growls. "Take me off speaker, Landon."

After a series of *uh-huhs* and *mmhms* end with a cartoony salute, Landon ends the call.

"Well?" I pry.

"You're nosy." Landon sends me a side-eye. "But lucky for you, I like sharing tea."

The man loves to gossip.

He lowers his head. Wade closes our small circle.

"Apparently, she can't afford her place anymore. She keeps taking on subleases and downsizing every few months. We offer to help out, but she refuses to borrow money from anyone, including her parents."

"Well, fuck." Wade nods. "That *sucks*."

My heart nearly breaks.

I would've never guessed she had any sort of trouble with...anything, really. Everything seems so easy, breezy, and relaxed for her.

Landon sighs. "Alright, I gotta get washed up."

My shower is anything but relaxing, as I think about Behraz struggling financially. The world is tough enough. I'd get rid of her troubles in a heartbeat if I could. But like I said, she doesn't know I exist. And I don't even really know her, right? It's a crush.

Yeah, a silly crush.

When I get back to my apartment, the loneliness subsides a bit, though I'm completely alone.

My bed is all too inviting. A book on my nightstand tempts me, and I retreat, losing myself in a world where the meek side character musters the courage to fight for the love of his life, ultimately saving himself.

Maybe one day I'll be able to do the same. Until then, I'll dream about Behraz Irani.

CHAPTER 2:
THE DEEPEST OF SHIT

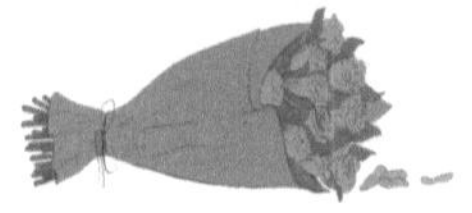

BEHRAZ

May

THE INNER MACHINATIONS OF MY BRAIN ARE AN ENIGMA.
However, unlike Patrick Star, there are simultaneously multiple things going on and absolutely nothing. No movement forward.

One part visualizes a milk carton toppling over and spilling its contents out, an image from a SpongeBob SquarePants episode that has been etched into my brain forever. Another grapples with a specific article that is currently giving me heartburn.

Professor Doherty's instructions are always so ambiguous. I think I follow them, right? But she originally stated that cases should be in-text citations. Then later, in person, she said, "No, you do them in footnotes, too." And I don't want to rewriggle my footnotes for the cases I put together, because I already put them in text citations. Like, I put them in-*text*. Everything else is footnotes. I was supposed to do one statute and at least three cases. I did two—*two*—statutes and *at least* five cases. On top of the background information and facts, and all of that.

And in the end, I wrote a fucking article, didn't I? I wrote a publishable article that explored the nuances of journalism, immigration, and cross-border conflict, and I did it pretty neatly. If I were to rate myself, I would say I gave a beautiful performance. And not only that, but this lady also says it has to be fifteen pages *exactly*. No more, no less. She says she'll grade me down if my analysis isn't perfect. I crashed out about this paper for three days in a row. Isn't that enough?

This is publishable material, but I'm not going to do shit with it. I'm never going to let this document see the light of day after I hand it over. I don't know how to feel. I should feel proud or whatever, but, *ugh*, I feel bad. I'm in this weird, limbo, middle zone because I worked really hard on it. It's well done. It's fifteen pages, with almost sixty citations and a really nuanced take on immigration law, but also the ways in which the government tries to delegitimize it by using terrorism. I thought she would like it, but the feedback on my last article was lackluster.

"It's too broad."

Mleh mleh mleh mleh mleh mleh.

Well, is it narrow enough for you yet? I focused this document's scope to hell, and now I'm so tired—

"Behraz?"

Oh, right. That's the third part. Paying attention to my mentor.

"I know it's a lot to take in."

Uh oh. I missed something. Which is on-brand for me, honestly. A woman meets with her mentor to discuss her academic woes and can't even stay focused.

"Sorry, I lost you." I sent her a nervous smile. "Could you repeat the last part?"

The worried wrinkle between Dr. Ahmad's stunning eyebrows deepens. "The results of the assessment, Miss Irani." Her tone is kind, but firm as always. "Along with your difficulties in processing written language, you have moderate to severe ADHD."

I laugh, which shocks her. What else am I supposed to do? The fact that it took me two months and twelve tries to finish the assessment should have been a pretty heavy indicator.

My throat clears, and I straighten. "So now what?"

Her perfect brows rise slightly. "There are a few things. I know a clinical psychologist on the faculty who specializes in ADHD in adult women. Dr. Sharon Gill. It would benefit you to work with her, figure out a course of therapy or treatment, and possibly get a referral to a psychiatrist, in the case you need a prescription or—"

"Right, right."

Therapy. Treatment. Meds. Got it.

"Then you can ask for accommodations from the Law Society of

Ontario, based on what Dr. Gill recommends..."

Is she sure I'm not just stupid? Like, who fails an open-book exam three fucking times?

"...You can take the exam again, you know? If they agree to the accommodations—"

"If—?"

"There's a whole process. It is a bit involved, but—"

Of course, it is. Why would anything be straightforward?

Maybe I'm not meant to be a lawyer. Maybe I should go back to being a legal secretary. I was decent at it. It wasn't terrible money. At least I could afford rent.

"I know you can do it, Behraz." Dr. Ahmad leans toward me, sliding over a file containing the assessment results. "You're incredibly intelligent, and you could be an outstanding lawyer if you want to be." She pauses, concern weathering her expression. "Take the help, Miss Irani."

"I appreciate you saying that. Thanks." I collect the folder and tuck it into the vintage-style brown leather briefcase I splurged on before law school.

She checks her watch and stands. "I'll email you Dr. Gill's contact information after my next meeting."

I'm halfway down the street when I realize I forgot to ask her what this would cost. The school covered the assessment, but what about the rest of it? My savings account has already been hemorrhaging from this ridiculous career dream of mine.

I swing the bag into the basket of my propped bike against the rack. My hand gets stuck while I'm fishing my keys from my jeans pocket to unlock it, and when I finally remove it with a grunt, the force of my pull launches it across the path, slapping an innocent passerby on the face.

The man is too stunned to speak.

"Oh, shit. I'm so sorry." My feet betray me, tripping over themselves when I scramble to grab the keys from the cement. I faceplant. Or boob-plant rather. Right over his shoes.

"Jesus," he mumbles.

"Sorry, sorry." I skitter back on my knees, waiting for him to move so I don't somehow take him out when I stand. Spatial awareness isn't my strong suit, and fresh bruises are evidence of it.

I can accept that some days are worse than others, but the days when nothing in my life goes right seem to be increasing. I unlock my bike with a sigh. And right on cue, it starts raining.

Of course, I don't have an umbrella. Or a raincoat.

The ride through puddles is atrocious, and by the time I pull up to my apartment, I'm thoroughly drenched, a strip of wet dust and debris streaked up my back, despite the splatter guard. I'll have to stop by the laundromat tomorrow. I haul my bike through the doorway, and the heavy wood and glass door slams while I park behind the stairs.

My sneakers squish every step of the way to the third floor. The sweat and rainwater combo does not smell great on me.

Zoe and her boyfriend, Alan, glare at me over their coffee mugs when I step through the apartment door.

What a nice, warm welcome.

I pretend not to see them past the shroud of dripping hair covering my face and make a beeline to my bedroom, but it's a no-go.

Alan nudges Zoe with an elbow.

"Hey, *Bea!* We wanted to talk to you about something," she starts.

"Oh, hi!" I chirp, splitting the wet strands apart and pushing them behind my ears. "What's up?"

My roommate motions to the empty chair across from them at the round kitchen table. "I know these past few months have been rough..."

"But they're rough on Zoe, too," Alan interrupts.

She squeezes his forearm to silence him. "I knew we discussed it, but I can't keep covering your half of the rent."

I'd argue my case, but it's too embarrassing to mention the amount of money left in my bank account. My savings have been wholly gouged. "It's only been a couple of months, and I was gonna reach out to the law firm I used to work for about getting some part-time work—"

The explanation is ignored.

"We were already kinda planning to move in together when your sublease was up. Alan is gonna pay for the last two months—"

"Oh, gosh, that's really generous, but—"

"If you move out."

"Move out?" Where would I go? I mean, I could figure it out. I've always figured it out. Say yes, Behraz. You won't owe rent. Find another sublease for even cheaper until you get all this bar exam business outta the way and then—

"By the end of the month."

My jaw hangs.

"*This* month? Like, in two weeks?"

"Yeah."

Now, I'm in shit. The deepest of shit. Okay, okay. You got this. You don't have that much stuff. Get it together. This is probably for the best.

"Okay."

They seem pleased. I go to my room to peel away my wet clothes and shower, making a mental list of things that I need to get done. One, write all this down. I step into the tub and turn the faucet on.

There's no hot water.

I want to cry. But I don't.

Instead, I text Indi. She's the closest thing I have to family left in this city.

ME

Hey, my hot water isn't working. Can I come over to shower?

INDI BHINDI

Again? You need to move outta that dump.

If only she knew.

INDI BHINDI

But yes, come over!! You know you don't have to ask.

INDI BHINDI

I was just gonna text you because we ordered way too much pizza

ME

Be there in 15

INDI BHINDI

Also don't judge me for the state of my house

I'd be the biggest hypocrite if I did that, considering how I keep my bedroom.

Today, however, Landon and Indi's place looks like the inside of my brain.

"Don't say anything," Indi warns.

I nearly topple over while untying my sneakers at the door and taking in the disarray. The usually spotless living space of their massive penthouse is filled with multiple giant suitcases. They lie open, half-packed with nuts, Costco-size packs of chocolate bars, and diapers. Indi leads the way, navigating through the maze toward an open spot.

Their dining table has become a khajano of Indian clothes: heavily beaded kurtas, sherwanis, anarkali-style gowns, and lehengas drape over the backs of each chair. One chair with Akhila-sized lehengas makes me audibly *awww*.

A variety of colorful jooti lie in a pile on the floor beneath the bar overhang of the kitchen island, its countertop smattered with stacks of brocade-covered jewelry boxes and clear-film packed sleeves of bangles.

"What in the name of Bollywood is happening here?"

My friend reclines on the sectional and soundlessly places a palm on her forehead while staring off into the ceiling. "This is called 'traveling internationally with a one-year-old to celebrate your baby sister's wedding—"

Oh yeah, Esha's getting married this summer.

"But your parents are so obsessed with their first grandchild that they want to throw her *another* over-the-top birthday party in India while all the family is together."

Reason #549 why I shouldn't have children. I can't even remember to pack my own toothbrush, much less anything and everything required for an entire human who is entirely dependent on you for survival.

"So...much...stuff." My eyes scan the room.

"We're leaving in two days, and I'm terrified we'll leave something behind."

"I'm sure you can find anything you want there."

She lets out a heavy breath through her nose. "You're right."

It'd be the first time.

"India has everything now, right? That's what I'm told, anyway."

Her eyebrow perks. "You should go sometime. It's so different than when I was a kid."

"Maybe one day."

It's weird being a third-culture kid and having almost no ties to your ancestral home. I imagine that's how the old generations of many Indian Parsis felt. Tanzania and Muscat felt more like home than Mumbai.

"How's your family, by the way? Are Sano Aunty, Barjor Uncle doing good now that your brother's with them?"

"Oh, yeah. They love having him there. They're living their best lives."

I've done an excellent job hiding the bitterness in my tone, because she seems to miss it. They're having a grand ol' time without me. Without their problem child.

"Very nice."

"Anyway, where's my little bacchu? I wanna squish her chunky cheeks."

"Landon's giving her a bath before bedtime." Her hand slides to cover her face. "You can squeeze her cheeks tomorrow. It's witching hour, and she'll shriek like a banshee if we screw up the routine. *God*, I'm so tired."

Oh, right. That's why I came over.

"I should go shower, too."

"You know where to go."

I feel bad for asking, but I don't wanna go home.

"Would it be okay for me to stay the night?"

Indi peeks through her fingers. "What's going on? Is everything okay?"

Everything is not even close to being okay. But I can't seem to tell her that what we thought was a learning disability is actually full-fledged ADHD, and that I'm getting kicked out of the apartment they helped me move into three months ago.

"My roommate—" is all I can manage.

"Is she being an asshole?"

Yes, but I can't tell Indi about their ultimatum either. She'd call Gabe, and they'd go fight Zoe in the alley or something. Those two are fiercely protective of their loved ones. And they can be scary. Maybe it's their height. Every short girl needs a tall best friend and vice versa. I'm not above stabbing their enemies. I guess I'm protective of them, too.

They've been through so much these past few years. And they don't need me to burden them with my problems. They have grown-up lives, partners, and families to worry about.

"No, no. Nothing like that. It's just...her boyfriend is staying over tonight, and—"

I can't get myself to tell her everything.

"And you don't wanna hear 'em bang?"

That, too. Now I don't have to lie so much.

"Yeah." I laugh nervously. "It's gross."

She frowns. "Well, you can stay as long as you want. We leave in two days, but you know you're welcome to stay here anytime, Bea." Her free hand finds mine and squeezes before letting go. "You're family."

My heart clenches. I fight back fat, hot tears until they can be drowned out by the whir of the fan and cascade of their fancy rainfall shower head.

I feel a little better after the hot shower and a good cry.

Weak, lamenting moans trickle into the guest room from beneath the door. I'm not about to walk in on my best friend having private adult time, but I can't help but poke my head out and peek down the hallway.

Nope, nothing there.

The noises get louder as I near the living room.

I spot Landon with both hands palming his head. He groans and rubs his face.

Indi stands facing him, arms crossed.

"What happened?"

She finally notices me. "No big deal, just my husband being reckless and juvenile."

"Baby," he whines.

"Don't '*baby*' me, Radek."

I gasp. She used his maiden name. He winces.

"Apparently, the boys don't play poker during the season to avoid losing too much money. But now, since they're out of the playoffs, they thought it'd be a good idea to gamble their sadness away."

Who can blame them? They kinda blew it this year. And last year.

"And they knew—*they knew!*—Fletcher would clean them out and wipe the floor with 'em."

Fletcher?

Fuck me, Fletcher Donovan.

In my dreams, he does.

Just the sound of his name has me tensing, sexually. Physically, there's a tear rolling down my thigh.

The man is perfection. You know when you see someone so hot, you can tell they smell good? Yeah, that's Fletcher Donovan. And I know for a fact he does. God, he smells incredible. I once caught a whiff of him when I passed by him in the family waiting area of a birthing center where Indi had Akhila, and it altered my brain chemistry. I can't pinpoint exactly what he smells like, but it's that fresh out of the shower, soapy clean. They say God doesn't choose favorites, but that's a lie, because Fletcher exists.

I wanna lick those beautiful freckles off his beautiful face. And those meaty, toned arms. I'd apply to be his hockey helmet only to tug his pretty red hair and take a ride on his face all damn day. And his voice? I wanna drink it down like Ursula from The Little Mermaid.

Alright, get it together, Bea. The man has you going full-Disney villain and getting all riled up with no plan in place for relief. Good thing no one can read my mind. It's filthy in here.

"He doesn't have a tell! What are we supposed to do?" Landon argues.

Her hands fly up. "Quit playing poker with him, god damn it!" His *hmph* ends in a pout and crossed arms like a petulant child. "Stick to the sport, okay, hockey boy?"

"Fine," he mumbles and holds out his hands, grabbing for her. "Do I still get cuddles?"

Knife, meet back.

I am so fucking single.

Indi rolls her eyes and tilts her head to the right. "Get in the bedroom."

I clap my hands together. "Don't have to tell me twice."

The joke doesn't land as well as expected, and I back up, retreating to my room for the night. I'm lucky they didn't boo or throw tomatoes.

I let the bed swathe me, burrowing into the luxurious sheets and fluffy comforter like a warm hug.

You're family, she said. Worst comes to worst, at least I know I can crash here temporarily. But it won't come to that. I try affirmations and flood my thoughts with positivity.

I can do this.

Something has to work out.

CHAPTER 3:
IS THIS HEAVEN?

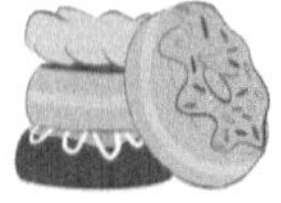

FLETCHER

June

TREATING MYSELF TO A STOP AT MY FAVORITE BOOKSTORE on the way back home from a run doesn't cure me of the constant tinnitus of Behraz's name in my head.

Black Squirrel Books on Bank St. is my newest haunt. Their shelves are always stocked, the espresso bar is brilliant, plus, the girl behind the counter, Belle, always has the best book recs. And sometimes they have these carrot cake doughnuts that have me questioning my loyalty to SuzyQ. Nah, that'd never happen. That place gives me a reason to live.

I walk away with three of her suggestions and an iced latte, but can't resist swinging past SuzyQ for one of their classics, a D'OHnut. It's vanilla, dipped entirely in a glaze, covered in sprinkles and tastes like summer.

One large sip washes down the crumbs and I frown at the caloric intake, knowing I'll pay for it when we begin training later in the summer. My mind replays a conversation with Wade from the day before.

"You gonna be okay without us until dry land training?"

"I'm a grown-up." I made a sarcastic face at him through the screen. "So, yes."

"Hey, I'm just checking. This is the first year in a long time you're not going home, Landon and Indi are gone, and we're leaving tomorrow morning."

"*Your point?*"

"*Dude, you have no other friends.*"

Ouch. True, but still, ouch.

"*And?*"

"*Unless you count your cock.*"

"*Shut up.*"

"*Like, what are you gonna do for the next two months by yourself? There's only so many hours of the day you can jerk off.*"

My expression went flat, middle finger slowly appearing in front of the phone camera. "*I'm gonna get a shit ton of reading done.*"

"*Oh, good. So, you'll be reading and jerking off.*"

"*I'm gonna hang up now.*"

"*Wait—speaking of...*"

"*I overheard Gabe talking to Indi about Bea. She's staying in Ottawa for the summer.*"

I knew that. Because I'm a weirdo stalker who scrolls through her social media any chance I get.

"*Oh, right.*" I shrugged it off. "*I think I saw her at Akhila's first birthday party or something.*"

And in every wet dream I've had for the past six years.

"*You saw her, alright. You were practically drooling. Now all you have to do is get over yourself and talk to her.*"

"*Yeah, okay.*"

He wasn't convinced. "*Come on, dude. You've had a hard-on for her for years.*"

I ignored him.

"*This is your lucky summer. I can feel it.*"

Luck? Who's she?

"*Sure, bud. Whatever you say.*"

"*Alright, well, don't be mad when she ends up with someone else.*"

My teeth grated together. I felt sick to my stomach. Every time I saw other men talk to her, make her laugh, touch her, dance with her, I thought my head would explode from jealousy. I had no right to be, but it didn't matter.

Wade must've noticed the red crawling up my cheeks.

"*Ugh, fine. Be that way. Sor-ry if I wanna see my friend hap-*

pily getting laid."

"Pervert," I deflected, "you'd enjoy seeing that wouldn't you?"

His hands lifted in an exasperated shrug. "I'm only a man."

"Oh-kay...anyway, I've got to be going now. Y'know, these books aren't going to read themselves. Have fun in Florida. Don't touch the dinosaurs."

"You're welcome to join anytime. We can go hit a few golf balls..."

No, thank you. The last time the team went down to his place in Fort Lauderdale, I got burned to a crisp. My skin peeled for weeks.

"I'll let you know."

A text notification flashes on screen, pulling me back to the moment.

TWINNY

You don't have to listen to Parker, you know

TWINNY

You can still come home

ME

I know, Mills

ME

I just don't feel like it right now

TWINNY

Valid

TWINNY

Seriously, come whenever. We miss you.

ME

Thanks

I wander down the footpath through the speckled shade from old trees lining the waterfront. My slow pace has dog walkers, joggers, and cyclists passing me every couple of minutes.

The breeze off the canal makes it feel cooler than it is, and I shiver, sweaty t-shirt still damp from the short 5k run.

A bike bell rings in the distance, contrasting with the rustle of the brown paper bag holding the newest additions to my book collection and the crackle of ice in my coffee. In the distance, a Behraz-shaped figure whizzes along the path.

Nah, it can't be. She doesn't even live over here.

I wait at the pedestrian crossing even though there are no cars. The red DON'T WALK sign taunts me. Come on, come on. No one's on the road. Just cross. Be a man. No one ever died because they jaywalked. A few moments go by.

Fuck it.

One cautious step onto the street and a car honks as it drives by at full speed, and I return to the curb. Jesus. Where did that come from? I glance to the right. Then the left. Okay, now there's really no one. Once more, I look to the right to make sure, before stepping down to the white stripes on the road.

Tring-tring!

The next few seconds draw out in slow motion. A shrill scream. Impact. The collision knocks the air from my lungs, but the freefall that follows feels like it's happening to someone else. At least until the back of my head hits the pavement.

When my eyes reopen, there's a blurry shower of rose petals and paper. Is this Heaven?

The throbbing in my ears drowns out any other noise, and I gasp, each breath further out of reach.

And then there is contact. I focus on the face hovering over me. Creamy skin. A beauty spot topping her left cheek.

Behraz.

Oh, God. This *is* Heaven. She's an angel. Flushed, cherubic cheeks, head haloed by the sun. The soft ends of her hair tickle my face. And those eyes—*her big, dark, gorgeous brown eyes*—they warm with concern. Warm like a much-needed sunny day in spring before the midsummer rays get too hot for my pale skin.

Speaking of hot, what's on my chest? Her hands? *Fuck*, they're on my chest. She's touching me, her small, delicate hands unable to cover my pecs. Fuck, she's touching me all over, *fuck*. If I'm not dead already, this is what will kill me.

Every panicked sweep of her hands feels better than the last. My hands reach for her wrists, so tiny and warm, gripping them as if begging for her to stop, though I don't want her to.

Oh no, no, no. My dick stirs as my vision darkens. I'm gonna pass out.

Please, God. Don't let me pass out in front of Behraz Irani with a boner.

Pain and anguish tug at whatever thread I'm holding onto, and my throat lets out a whimper.

The stripes of her shirt disappear in the lines of light stealing my vision. Bea's rosy face pinholes into darkness, and suddenly, there's no more pain.

CHAPTER 4:
HE'S NOT DEAD

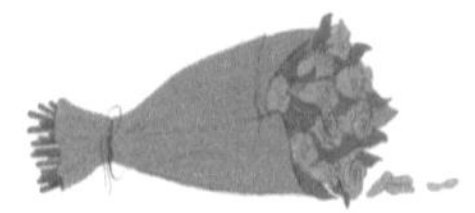

BEHRAZ

OH, MY GOD, I'VE KILLED FLETCHER DONOVAN.

Fuck, fuck, fuck. *Fuck*!

"Help! Someone call 9-1-1!" I cry and search for my phone. My bicycle lies sideways in the middle of the road, rose bouquet all but destroyed, the contents of my briefcase strewn down the block.

I can't move from here. I can't leave him. He's out cold, and besides, his grip still clings to my hands.

"Please wake up. Please, please, please wake up." My ear sinks to his chest. His heart beats rapidly. The short, quick exhalations from his nose cool my sweat-dotted forehead.

Okay, he's not dead. Thank God.

"Now, you've gone and done it, Bea. You fucked up royally," I mutter to myself.

A woman with her puppy taps me from behind. "The ambulance is on the way."

"Thank you so much—I don't know where my phone is, and..." Manic sobs pour from me over his stilled form.

I don't want to let him go when it arrives but am forced to when the paramedic straps Fletcher to a stretcher and loads him into the back.

"Can I go with him?" I ask as they place an oxygen mask on his face.

"If you'd like."

"Ma'am?" A police officer stands behind me with my dinged-up bike and scraped-up belongings. "Is this yours?"

"Yes." I collect my things from him before turning back to the ambulance. "I need to ask you some questions."

"But I'm going with them to the hospital. Can we do that when we get there?" My voice shakes as I lock the bike to a sturdy signpost nearby and throw my bag over my shoulder. "I'm not leaving him."

"You know one another?" the policeman asks.

Who in this town doesn't know Ottawa's redheaded sweetheart? Landon and Wade are fun and charming, but they're also very taken.

Fletcher Donovan, on the other hand, is the most beautiful man I've ever set eyes on. Millions of single women across Canada would agree.

"He plays for the Regents."

"Miss, I meant, do you know him personally?"

Honestly, I don't. But I wish I did. I'd like nothing better than to know Fletcher Donovan.

"Sorta, it's complicated." I brush the question off as the paramedic helps me climb into the ambulance and seats me across from Fletcher.

The shock wanes, and my eyes brim with saltwater. As if he can sense it, his eyes roll open to look at me.

Fletcher looks terrified. His hand blooms open weakly. I reach for it.

"I'm so sorry," I weep, sandwiching his hand between mine. "I'm so, *so* sorry."

The corner of his full, ashen lips lifts into a frail smile before his heart monitor beeps wildly and he loses consciousness again.

———

I hug my arms, rubbing the goosebumps away in this freezing hallway of Ottawa Hospital General.

So much has happened in the past few hours. Fletcher woke up long enough to tell his side and graciously informed the police officer, named Owens, that he didn't want to file charges.

Yet he doesn't say a word to me.

Judging by how red his face is, I bet he's furious. Concussions mean you can't play. Maybe it doesn't matter since the Regents are no longer in the playoffs. Still, he's probably pissed that he won't be able to do the things he usually does as a professional athlete.

Great job, Behraz. I mentally give myself a slow clap while checking the clock on the wall.

Sitting alone in a room in silence with Fletcher Donovan is insanely awkward. I need to get outta here, but the nurse said the doctor wants to speak to me about something. Not sure what it could be, but—

There's a knock at the door.

"Come in," Fletcher answers quietly.

"Hi there, I'm Dr. Chhabra." A balding middle-aged physician enters. "You look terrible."

Everyone's a comedian.

Fletcher returns a fake laugh. I recognize it's fake because I've heard his real one on the team's TikTok account. Usually forced out by Wade Boehner, their prankster goalie, or their social media manager trolling his teammates.

She once recorded their reactions to her calling them pookie, and the blush on Fletcher's face had me fanning myself. I'd simply pass away if I could make him blush like that. And then I'd come back to life to do filthy, unspeakable things to him.

I blink errantly, bringing myself back to reality and Dr. Chhabra explaining concussion protocol.

"Is there anyone you can call to stay with you for the next two weeks while you recover? Family?"

"Not family," Fletcher replies.

"Maybe a friend," I interject, lowering my voice to a whisper when the golden hues of Fletcher's eyes lock with mine. "Or a teammate."

"It's the offseason. They're all on vacation."

Oh, right. Landon and Indi are in India for Esha's wedding and Akhila's second-first birthday party. And Wade and Gabe went to Florida.

"There's no one?" the doctor asks.

Fletcher shrugs, pushing an ache into my chest. Does he really have no one else?

"What about you?"

I gape at the doctor and rest a finger on my sternum. "Me?"

"Yeah. Officer Owens said you knew each other."

"I mean, 'know' is pretty loosely defined here." The thought of living with the man of my dreams catches me off guard. And nervous. And when

I'm nervous, I ramble. "Like, yes, he's my friend's husband's teammate, so 'we know each other'"—my fingers form air-quotes—"but who really knows anyone in this vast ocean of life?"

Dr. Chhabra lifts a curious eyebrow. He's speechless.

Fletcher pushes out a deep sigh, visibly exhausted. "She can stay with me."

My eyes widen and widen further when he subsequently falls asleep.

"It's settled then."

"No offense, Doctor. But I have no idea how to care for someone in this...situation."

"Absolutely no worries. He's severely concussed, but he's going to be fine. I'll have a nurse go through the protocol with you. And can connect you with someone who can check on him at home."

I guess it is settled then.

I'll be living with Fletcher Donovan for two weeks.

CHAPTER 5:
THE SUBJECT OF MY OBSESSION HAS BEEN LIVING IN MY HOUSE

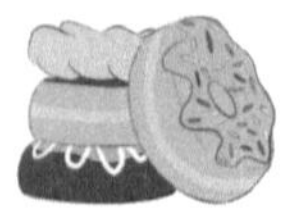

FLETCHER

WADE WAS RIGHT.

All I'll be doing this summer is reading and jacking off.

Between this concussion and Behraz Irani traipsing around my apartment in those tiny, flouncy dresses, my head's gonna implode.

The first two days are absolute torture. I can't get out of bed without feeling nauseated or disoriented, or both. The room spins every time I stand, and I'm not sure if it's from the brain injury or Behraz holding me up. She's surprisingly strong, considering I'm probably a foot taller and at least seventy pounds heavier. I'm goaded back into bed each time with a shush.

My temporary roommate seems to be both ever-present and absent. I barely see her, but I smell her goddamn rose perfume everywhere. It's intoxicating and infuriating.

All the while, I don't have to worry about anything else but healing. Not sure if Behraz called her friends or my teammates, or if Landon sent a cleaning crew and Wade asked his private chef to come over, but dirty laundry disappears and returns to my closet clean and folded, and the fridge and pantry are fully stocked. Like clockwork, thoughtful meals appear in the kitchen. Avocado toast, topped with sliced hard-boiled eggs. Hot oatmeal with walnuts and seeds. Salmon with sweet potatoes and green beans. Blueberry smoothies and lemony kale salads with cranberries and cilantro dressing so good I want to bathe in it.

And don't get me started on the hearty stew served with brown rice and a cucumber salad. It has lentils and veggies, some type of fish, and is spiced so perfectly, I swear it brings me back to life.

I'm gonna have to thank the chef, because I go from struggling through a slow walk across the room to a steady jog along the canal in a matter of days. No sign of headache, either.

I laugh through panted breaths and clap once in victory before heading back home. Fourteen days have gone by in a blur, and I made it through.

Tomorrow, I'll attempt a trip to the gym, I tell myself while entering the apartment and slipping off my sneakers.

But I'm not prepared for what awaits me. Or who, rather.

Behraz Irani is curled up on the couch with all the blackout curtains drawn. A picked-at take-out container of poutine and a half-empty handle of whiskey sit on the coffee table.

She's still here? The homecare nurse already cleared me. Maybe she feels guilty, but it's not a big deal. Concussions are practically in the job description of professional hockey players.

For two weeks, I barely survived her curious brown eyes peeking through the door to check on me. Two weeks of stolen glances across the living area, when exiting our rooms, were too close for comfort. But now? There's no avoiding her.

Music plays from the large TV. Subtitles sit at the bottom of the screen as a woman stands in the middle of a field, drenched from the rain and visibly crying. The camera pans to a scene at a temple where another woman dressed in traditional Indian clothing wails while dancing to a folksy, heart-wrenching tune into the clouds above her. Definitely the type of Bollywood movie Landon and Wade watch all the time. Those two are obsessed.

Obsessed? I'm one to talk. Or not talk.

The subject of my obsession has been living in my house, and I haven't managed to say a word to her. She's right here, and yet, I don't dare to open my mouth.

A chunky knit pink blanket drapes over her head and shoulders, the panels held together at her chest like a burrito. She shifts. Curiosity gets the best of me, and I inch closer to the couch to get a better view of the TV. Then Behraz sniffles. My throat clears, not by any intention of my own, and it catches her attention.

She gasps out a sob and whips her head to me.

Streaked tears stain her reddened cheeks. Usually bright, brown eyes cloud with pain.

Something breaks. It's my heart.

"Oh," I say aloud.

Behraz leaps up from her seat and launches onto me, wailing. I nearly lose my footing when her arms circle my neck, damp tears smearing the chest of my t-shirt.

It nearly killed me the first time Behraz Irani touched me like this. And not just because of the bicycle crash. Her hands on me, *God*, they feel as close to paradise as possible. My entire body goes stiff. Both hands twitch, wanting to rid her of whatever hurt she's feeling. She deserves comfort.

You don't have words, Fletch, but you can do this.

I soften and wrap her in a hold, lifting her until her face buries in my shoulder. Her loose, dark hair surrounds me, full, lush, and silken. The cotton of her pants swishes against the exposed skin covering my knees. She continues to wrack through heavy sobs as I lower us until we're seated on the couch.

I should stop thinking about how good she feels. So soft and warm. Need to stop breathing the delirium-inducing smell of roses from her skin and saltwater from her tears. It has my nervous system in pieces. Need to ignore how close we are, how my heart is almost touching hers. But god-damn, I'm a selfish bastard. I don't want to stop.

"I'm"—she snivels through the trickle of snot between her cute little nose and tempting set of pink lips—"so...*sorry*!" Her face returns to my collarbone, tight grasp moving from my neck to fisting my shirt. I angle my hips away from her, afraid the contact will signal my half-hard cock to move into phase two. She lifts her head and glances up, expression painted with turmoil. "I messed up! Everything is all messed up!"

"Uh?" My armpits sweat with a fury.

"No matter how hard I try"—her head sways against me in disbe-lief—"nothing goes right in my life."

So, we have something in common.

"I failed the bar exams *three* times. It's an open textbook exam! The answers are right in front of my eyes, and I still can't get it done on time. I've been beating myself up, like, how can I be so stupid?"

You're not, I want to say, but nothing comes out. I keep quiet and listen.

"Turns out, I'm not stupid. Nope. I have a learning disability and ADHD, and the time constraint is the reason I haven't been able to pass. And it's all so expensive! The exam, the ADHD assessment, the therapy. So, of course, I'd get kicked out of my sublease—"

Wait, what? Kicked out?

"My roommate's boyfriend took it over and paid the back rent I owed. I guess I should be thankful I don't have to pay for it. I wish I could go back to my brother's place, but he moved to Muscat with my parents. I sold my piece of shit car because I couldn't afford gas or insurance or to fix it up all the time. I'm closer to thirty than twenty, and I ride a banged-up city bike with a fucking basket on it all around Ottawa like a primary schoolgirl. I have no money, no place lined up to live next, and I haven't told anyone because everyone already thinks I'm a clumsy, absent-minded fuck-up. Admitting all this to them would just be the cherry on the shit sundae. They'd know what a fucking broke-ass failure I am."

Behraz takes a shaky inhale before continuing.

"I thought I could figure it out myself, then I ran you over. And no one's here. Everyone's gone, living their perfect fucking lives, and I'm here, alone. Completely fucking alone, trying to make sure you don't die and you"—there's a brief pause to rise from my shoulder and release a few more tears before she forces eye contact again—"why do you hate meeee?"

"I"—can barely get out the words—"don't?"

Short sobs staccato her words like hiccups. "Then"—sob—"why"—sob—"won't"—sob—"you"—sob—"talk"—sob—"to"—sob—"me?"

Oh, God. This poor girl thinks I hate her because I have the biggest crush on her and can't seem to piece together more than two words whenever she's around.

"Because I suck."

Three words. Progress.

I'm surprised she could even hear me over it, but her wailing quiets. She pushes herself away from my chest, and I reactively free her from the hold. "What?"

My hands find each other between my knees, knuckles cracking as I fidget with them. Heat creeps up my neck. My tongue goes lax, pretending to be dead when put on the spot in these unexpected circumstances. "I'm...I'm not good with words."

"No shit," she mutters, wiping her cheeks with the back of her hand.

My knees clench around my entwined hands. "I'm sorry, too. *Um*, for everything."

Her hands fly to her face as she recoils to the corner of the sofa. "Oh, my God. No, *I'm* so sorry. I just physically assaulted and trauma-dumped on you." She sniffles. "You know what's crazy, though? We've been living together in this apartment for a couple of weeks. I've been doing your laundry and cooking you all sorts of meals from that list your doctor gave me—" She points to a piece of paper in the kitchen stuck to the fridge with a magnet. "Granny's dhansak recipe single-handedly got you outta the house with a clean bill of health."

"That was...all you?"

I don't think my own family has ever taken care of me like that.

"Yeah, silly. Who do you think? Your fairy godmother? It's the least I could do...considering I took you out. I mean, the team sent a young kid named Leo to help—"

"Oh. My PA."

"—But the poor guy was supposed to be on vacation. So, well...I felt bad enough, and basically asked him to help me order groceries and whatever you needed for a couple of weeks, and then sent him on his way. Between me and Nurse Linney, we had it covered."

"Wow, *um*. I didn't know."

"Anyway, what I meant to say was that we've been living together—*technically, I've been living out of my suitcase*—and though you've seen me have an embarrassing meltdown...we haven't been properly introduced." Behraz gets to her feet and straightens her worn-in, oversized University of Ottawa tee before extending a hand. "Behraz Irani. Most people call me Bea."

I stand, too, but afraid that towering over her makes her uncomfortable, I hunch my shoulders to accept the shake. "Fletcher Donovan."

A static shock sparks between us.

"Sorry," we say together.

Another blush sears my skin, this time going as high as the tips of my ears. We retake our spots on the sectional, the silence awkwardly filling the room.

"I'm sure you wanted no part of it, but now you know the fucked-up disaster that is my life," she resigns. "But I know so little about you."

One of my shoulders lifts in a half-shrug. "Other than you have Pokémon collectibles, some sort of intimate friendship with SuzyQ doughnuts, and have an insane collection of fantasy novels."

"That's...a pretty good summary."

Bea motions to the filled bookshelves to point out a Pokéball and a Customer-of-the-Month trophy from my favorite doughnut shop. "And that you'd rather have an almost-stranger take care of you instead of your family."

When the almost-stranger is the woman you've been fantasizing about for six years, and your family is a bunch of jerks? I think I made the right choice.

"It's complicated."

"Yeah?" She leans on a hand on the cushion next to me. My eyes follow the acute angle of her elbow up to her face. Her head tilts to the side, those goddamn eyes rounded with curiosity and concern. "Wanna talk about it?"

Not really. Not at all. But after these past two weeks, I owe her that much.

CHAPTER 6:
NOSY PARSI AUNTY IS HERE TO STAY

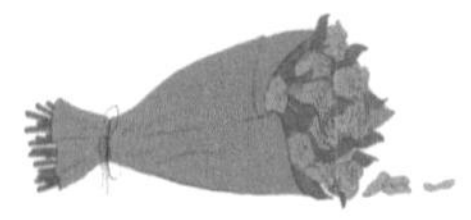

BEHRAZ

SITTING NEXT TO FLETCHER DONOVAN IS LIKE FLYING too close to the sun, except I don't mind having my wings burn away.

The warmth of his thigh against mine sets fire to the nervous butterflies in my stomach as he shows off a framed family picture. It's fucking huge. His family, I mean. His thigh, too, but that's beside the point.

There are twenty people posed on the front steps of a modest house. He's number five of seven, he says. I count four couples besides his parents and six nieces and nephews. All of his immediate family have shades of red hair, except for one head of medium-brown. Of the group, Fletcher has the most freckles, and his hair is the richest shade of auburn.

I fixate on the freckles dotting his muscled forearm holding out the photo. What would they taste like? What would *he* taste like? Probably as good as he smells, like soap and musky sweat. I could just, like, bend down and try. No, no. That's weird, Bea. Too weird, even for you.

"What do you wanna know?"

I gulp, ashamed of my unhinged train of thought.

"Who is everyone?"

"It's a lot...I don't expect you to remember."

"Try me."

It's my thing. I can remember names, faces, addresses. Feelings from the past I can't shake. Hundreds of cases and rulings alongside a plethora of random facts and figures. Got a memory like an elephant. Except, it seems, when I sit for a timed exam that my career depends on. Information vanishes from my brain as if I hadn't spent years studying the exact topic.

"My parents—Greg and Riona Donovan. Dad's a commercial fisherman. Mom works at a local grocery store in Summerside." He places his finger underneath each face in the top row. "Piper's the eldest, then Parker." Fletcher pauses. "He taught me how to play puck." I wonder about the rueful look in his eyes, but he answers it before I can pry. "I probably spent more time with Park than my dad," he admits.

"I'm sorry," I whisper, familiar with the pain of an absent parent. Or in my case, both parents.

"Of the two, Parker's the better option." He identifies two other older sisters, Greer, and Miller, who was born in the same year as him, and only eleven months older. "Then after me there's Harper, and Hunter's the youngest of all."

"Are you all close?"

A foghorn sounds out in my brain.

Make way! Nosy Parsi Aunty coming through!

His shoulders lift, unconvincing. "When we were growing up, yeah. Not so much anymore. My older sisters all have their own families. Harper lives on the west coast in Vancouver. Hunt is backpacking through eastern Europe this year."

"What about Parker?"

Nosy Parsi Aunty is here to stay.

Fletcher sighs through his nose. "We got into an argument."

"That's why you didn't want to call your family?"

His thumb stays put under his brother's face in the picture. "Park would have lost it."

"Ah," I say knowingly. "Older brothers."

He returns a slow nod, the corner of his mouth pinching into a frown.

"I've got one of those. He's super overprotective and annoying."

Fletcher's eyebrow perks. How did I manage to make this about me? *Self-centered*, my parents say. I guess I do it too often. My new ADHD therapist explained it's a form of masking. I'm afraid of not being relatable because I already worry that I'm not, and instead, offer up something similar from my life.

It's probably why I'm not great at making or keeping new friends. The behavior is either seen as narcissistic or sycophantic, and people get annoyed. But I can't help it. And Fletcher shows no sign of annoyance. So, I keep going.

"When I got rid of my car and bought a bike, he gave me a motorcycle helmet because he said I'm so clumsy, I'd get myself killed on the streets of Ottawa in a tragic bicycle accident." I fail to stifle my smile while eyeing Fletcher's response. "Little did he know…"

"*You* are Ottawa's infamous bicycle maimer." He's pulling back a smile, too.

I made Fletcher Donovan smile.

My heart soars, like Icarus, higher and higher, and ready to fall into the depths.

Get it together, Bea. It's only a crush.

The stupid beating organ has no desire to listen. My knee nudges his. "Hey, I said I was sorry about that." A beat hangs between us. Then two.

"I'm not." His gaze softens into mine, hazel hues going misty.

I think I might melt into this couch and onto the floor.

"Thank you, *um*, for everything."

My lips part in surprise.

"If you didn't stay…I would've been all alone, too." His confession reminds me of my own loneliness. "Hey, *um*, Behraz?"

"Seriously. You can call me Bea."

"Can I ask you something?" He places the family portrait face down on the coffee table. Anxiety courses through my veins, sending my heart rate into outer space. What is he gonna ask? People don't say that without it being serious. My face feels hot, but I try to play it cool.

"Sure."

Haziness changes to worry in his eyes.

"Do you really have no place to live?"

The air shifts. So, it is a serious question. I blink twice. I could lie and say that now he's back to himself and all good on his own, I'll be staying at Indi's or Gabe's while they're away. Just until I find a new apartment. I could lie and say I found a place, and I'll get out of his hair tomorrow morning. The truth is far too embarrassing, and I've already made a whole ass fool of myself by bawling like a newborn baby while trying to climb him like a tree.

"Bea."

My name whispered from his mouth sends a shiver down my spine, and the sudden seriousness in his tone has me wanting to disappear into the walls.

"Where's all your stuff?"

I toy with my bottom lip. "In a storage...of sorts."

CHAPTER 7:
YOU HAVE TO PROMISE NOT TO TELL

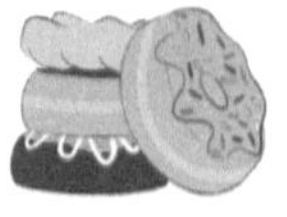

FLETCHER

BEHRAZ IRANI SIMULTANEOUSLY AND EQUALLY makes me nervous and at ease.

I'm genuinely surprised at how effortless it is to talk to her. There's still a pitter-patter in my belly, but at least I can be somewhat normal, comfortable enough to share a little.

I don't tell her about how Dad drinks. How out of control his gambling is. How the rest of my family can't cover my parents financially because they're barely getting by on their own. Or how I put Greer, Miller, Harper, and Hunter through university, though I couldn't go myself. And I'm too upset while piecing together her puzzle of woes to talk about why Parker and I fight.

Kicked out of her sublease. No money. No place to live. Living out of her suitcase.

I know I have no right to be, but I'm seething. Not at Behraz, but at the situation. How unfair, how heartless the universe is to throw such an unselfish, generous soul—*someone who's clearly struggling and still gives a crap about someone she barely knows*—basically out onto the street. And along with everything else?

I remember when Harper was diagnosed with ADHD after uni and how she struggled to manage it. She had a whole support system through work. All the siblings came through, even Park. Behraz doesn't even have family in the country. She must be terrified.

"You can stay here," I offer.

She glances away and winces. "I probably shouldn't."

Yeah, she doesn't wanna live with you, you loser.

"But you can."

"I can't afford it."

"Oh, that's okay."

"No, it's not. This is a really nice place."

"And it's paid off." The statement comes off more arrogant than I would have liked. "How long were you thinking?"

Her eyes go wide. "Maybe...two months? Only until I take my exam."

Two months? She can stay as long as she wants.

"Yeah, cool."

"I won't be able to pay rent now, or even a few months...but I *will* pay back when I can."

"It's fine. No worries."

It's not *fine*. I am a knotted ball of worries. I just invited Behraz Irani to live with me for two more months.

Oh, Fletcher. You're a sucker for punishment.

It might kill me to be around her so much.

"That's settled," I finalize, pushing myself off the sofa after clapping my knees. "Let's go get your things."

———

I should be paying attention to the road. Instead, I'm watching Behraz across the cab of my truck chewing on the skin of her thumbnail and staring through the lazy rain rapping against the window. The directions lead us to a strip shopping center on the other side of town, in Kanata, not far from the Regents home arena, the CTC.

We park next to the curb. The storefront signage is hidden by a white banner, the name and business hours half-scratched from the glass door, visibly closed in comparison to the lit-up neighboring Halal Butchers. The rickety wheels in my brain turn. I assumed Behraz was of Indian ancestry, like Indi and Gabe. Maybe she's Pakistani? Or Arab? I'm too unworldly to know for sure and asking her outright is surely a crime.

She keys open both locks with a heavy series of clicks and ushers me in behind her. "This is Gulabi Sweets," she explains, flicking on the lights.

"My brother's bakery. Or rather, it is until July 1st. The lease is almost up."

The air is stale, and the space is bare except for an askew glass cooler. There are some cobwebs settling in the corners of the rose-colored walls. Alternating black and white tiles pattern the floor.

"There used to be wicker tables and chairs throughout this area," she points out. "And that display was always filled. Trays of nan katai, soan papdi, baglu, butter biscuits, eeda pak, mawa ni boi, popatjee...all sorts of sweet and savory staples for a Parsi bakery."

The woman is saying words, but I have no idea what they mean. I'll have to do a Google deep dive of what a Parsi bakery is when we get home. I didn't think I was that ignorant, but I definitely don't know what Parsi means either.

"And the way it used to smell?" She inhales deeply and with content. "Parvez is a *really* good baker. He went to pastry school at Le Cordon Bleu."

Behraz walks to the back and pushes through a black swinging door, the kind that you see in movie restaurants. I follow her. We pass the empty kitchen and turn right. She twists the knob of a wooden door to reveal an office piled with boxes and trash bags.

"Ta da! It's mostly junk from over the years, but..."

Every single box is overflowing. Not a single one has been taped shut. Most of the giant garbage bags are overstuffed to the point they can't be cinched or tied. She only has a bike. My stomach churns thinking about how she hauled all of this on her own.

"How...how did you get it here?"

"It's not that much."

"It's more stuff than you could fit in your bike basket."

Her arms toss up in resignation. "Fine! You caught me. But you have to promise not to tell."

I rub a hand over my forehead. "Did you do something illegal?"

"Of course not! No," she says through a dismissive chuckle. "Sorta. Technically...yes."

Oh, boy.

"Promise," she urges.

"I promise."

"Swear to me." Her pinky extends to me. The woman has me swearing loyalty to her. As if she doesn't already have it. I hook my little finger into hers, cherishing the warm pressure of her tight hold.

"I pinky swear."

"I borrowed Landon's Range Rover."

I suck in a long breath. "*Borrowed*?" That's his most prized possession.

She hisses through her teeth in a cringe and releases our pinkies.

I zip my lips. "Yeah, that secret's going with me to the grave."

"It better, or" —she slices her thumb across her throat— "I can handle a knife. Plus, I'm notoriously prone to accidents."

My groin tightens. No, no, Fletch. This is not the time to be having dark fantasies about Behraz and all the things she could do to you with the edge of a sharp blade. I grab a trash bag and knot the top, holding it in front of me to hide a rapidly growing problem. "I'll start loading the truck."

When I return, Behraz kicks the bottom of a clay-stained pottery wheel. "It's too heavy."

I peek into a box of painted mugs and bowls sitting next to it. "Did you make these?"

"I don't know what I was thinking." Behraz shakes her head. "One whole summer, all I did was make and paint pottery. Thought it was gonna change my life or something."

"I mean, it's a cool hobby."

"I have, like, half a dozen abandoned hobbies. They're all 'cool.'" She pores through a few boxes. "I've got enough embroidery thread, cloth, and hoops to start a cross-stitching club. Nearly twenty skeins of yarn and countless lines of finger-knitted strands that were supposed to, I don't know, turn into sweaters or blankets, but I only made one blanket and didn't get anywhere after." Her index finger jabs angrily at a box that has its flaps tucked into one another. "This one has a collection of the New York Times's crossword puzzles. I only got through one book. Somewhere there's fancy art markers and stress-relieving Mandala coloring books for adults, too."

"My sister crochets," I offer, unprompted. "It helps her focus."

"That's why I started with this stuff. But I'm so unfocused." She interrupts herself by moving the box of crossword books. "I can't even focus on activities that are supposed to help me focus."

I pull the truck to the rear door and prop it open while she loads a box into the truck, and she returns the favor when I carry out the pottery wheel. She pauses after we're done, catching her breath while resting her hands on her hips. I struggle not to stare, but the dip of her waist and the swell of her chest under her oversized shirt have a vice grip around my attention.

When she turns...God help me, that ass. And don't get me started on the dewy pink flush on her cheeks.

"Where will I put all this crap in your apartment? I don't think it's gonna fit."

My mind is far too dirty and well-versed in fictional romance to steer clear of the suggestive wording. Hopefully, my face is red enough from loading boxes that she can't see me blush.

Don't say it'll fit. Don't say we'll make it fit.

"It can, *uh*, go in the spare room." Sweat trickles down my back, seeping through the cotton of my tee as I lay a tarp over the truck bed. "There are only a couple of bookshelves in there."

CHAPTER 8:
AM I READY TO LIVE WITH THIS STUNNING MAN FOR THE NEXT TWO MONTHS WITHOUT TOUCHING MYSELF TO DEATH?

BEHRAZ

"HEY, ARE WE FRIENDS NOW?"

Fletcher blushes so fiercely that it makes my heart skip a beat. The crimson spans all his exposed alabaster skin, drowning his freckles down his arms to the knuckles around the steering wheel. My stomach flips back and forth like a floor gymnast. A smile stretches my face so wide my cheeks hurt. Dreams do come true. I could get used to seeing him like this.

"S-sure."

"So, my friend. You're a shy bookworm who plays hockey professionally?" I tease.

"I...guess." He's still stumbling over words. I might be addicted to making him blush.

"Is reading your only hobby? Or are you like me, a hobby hoarder?"

His shoulders round into a shrug. "Hockey takes up most of my time. When we're not practicing or playing, we're on the road."

"No other hobbies? Really? What do you guys do during long trips?"

"Catch up on sleep. Watch movies. Sometimes we play card games."

"Fun! You mean like Uno?" I ask, though I already have insider info.

I want to, have to, *need* to make Fletcher Donovan smile. And maybe blush some more.

God forbid a girl has a new hobby. Add it to the list, the endless lists with tasks that never get completed, or if they do, are completed too late and it doesn't matter anyway. The domino effect of failure never fails.

"Occasionally. We usually stick to Phase 10, Pokémon—"

Gabe and Indi were right. These guys are giant children with geeky pastimes.

"Sometimes pinochle—"

"Pinochle?" I choke on a laugh. "What are you guys, eighty?"

Fletcher's mouth purses. He's really trying not to smile.

"If you must know, my favorite is poker. Texas Hold 'Em. But the guys aren't fans."

I've made him blush. I've made him smile, kinda. Now I wonder if I can get him to compliment himself.

"No? Why not?" That's good, Bea. Pretend you don't know about his poker skills.

"'Cause when they play, they bet. And when I play, they lose." A faint smile appears, changing the pattern of those pretty freckles.

Victory!

His smile stretches with mischief. "And men who play sports for a living are the biggest sore losers."

"*Daaaaang*, Fletcher," I sing-song. "How'd you get so good?"

The question hits a nerve, because he goes somber. "My dad plays." We stop at a red light, the right turn signal ticking through the silence. "It's probably the only thing he taught me." The hurt in the low timbre of his voice bristles my skin. A green glow tints his silhouette, and we drive forward.

"If it makes you feel any better, my parents are jerks, too." They hate me so much that they had to put seven thousand miles between us. I've made this about me again. How selfish. "Anywayyyyy," I sing, "I've never played. You'll have to teach me when we get back to your place."

"*Our* place."

My lips pull into a thankful smile, averting my eyes out of the window to hide my excitement. Luckily, he can't hear how fast my heart's beating.

This is the craziest turn of events.

I suck in a breath. "I can't believe I thought you resented me because you're shy." He blushes. Again. I swoon internally. I lick the tip of an imaginary pen and pretend to write on my palm like a notepad. "A shy, *nerdy* hockey player who reads and is a poker fiend. Family dynamics are complicated. Anything else I need to know, *roomie*?"

"I'm a simple man," he replies with an enigmatic smile as we turn into the apartment building's parkade.

"I doubt that." I tie my hair back into a ponytail, securing it with the black elastic on my wrist. He pulls into the designated spot, and we get down from the truck. The tailgate flips down with a soft bang. Reaching over it, he slides a box and picks it up as if it weighs nothing. There's no strain to his face or arms, but his sleeve stretches from the bulge of muscle flexing.

Yum.

My mouth waters when he turns and gives me a view of his perfect ass in those jeans.

"Ready?" he calls, tilting his head in the direction of the floor entrance.

It's my turn to blush. Which makes him blush. God, help me. Am I ready to live with this stunning man for the next two months without touching myself to death? Absolutely not. But I lie. I grab a trash bag with both hands. "Yep. Coming."

The spare room starts filling with my things, except for the boxes and bags that hold clothes. I transfer those to the bedroom. I don't let Fletch see the disaster contained within those four walls. I've told him about my ADHD, but he hasn't seen the damage firsthand, and it's too embarrassing to show him, even for me. I'll clean and organize in a hyperfixation panic later. I shut the door behind me and find Fletcher unpacking a box of my handmade mugs and placing them on the shelf with much nicer drinkware.

"Oh, you don't have to do that."

"Do what?"

"We don't have to use those."

"Why not?" His brows wrinkle together, eyes curious. "Did you use them before?"

"Well, yeah, but—"

"Then you can use them here." He studies the one that I painted a poop emoji on. It reads *poop juice*. I catch him smiling as he lifts it to the shelf. Yeah, he can do whatever he wants. "Plus, they're pretty funny. I like the naked banana one."

Fletcher Donovan thinks I'm funny? Hell yeah, I'm funny.

"You think so?" I beam, then brush it off.

I'm cool. Stay cool.

My hand flips the end of my ponytail over one shoulder. "I mean, I *am* the funniest of my friends."

"I don't know," Fletcher intones. "Gabe is hilarious."

I gasp, one hand splaying against my chest, faking scandal. "Oh, really? Why don't you go live with her then?"

The look on his face and the quirk of a corner of his full lips has wry mischief written all over it. "She already has a roommate. They're married, too."

"Ahhhh," I say with a slow, dramatic nod, crossing my arms over my chest. "So, I'm your second choice."

My joke falls flat. Fletcher's wide smile softens and disappears, as if I've offended him.

"You're no one's second choice."

Yeah, right. I've never been anyone's priority, not even for my family. Why'd he say that? What does that mean?

He turns his back to me while putting the last mug in the cupboard. I almost miss when he whispers, "And definitely not mine."

An uncomfortable pause hangs between us. I focus on the white trash bag filled with pots and pans on the counter and toy with one, spinning the handle in my grip.

"You can put those anywhere you want." Fletcher points to the cookware and the knife block next to it. "I meant it when I said this is your home, too." His fingers curl over the edge of the counter where he leans, shoulders slumped slightly. The lines of his lush lashes hide his downward gaze. "Even if it's temporary."

I must be reading it wrong, because he can't possibly be sad about the thought of me, an unbearable demon of chaos, who's disrupting and destroying his quiet life, getting out of his hair in two months' time. It doesn't make any sense. I'll figure him out later. Like everything else.

"Thanks, Fletcher." I pry open one of the lower cupboards and find some space alongside his pots and pans, then straighten. "I'm gonna sort through some things and get cleaned up before bed. I've got an early start tomorrow."

"Yeah? Where are you going?"

"Down the street from Parliament Hill. I told the old law firm I used to work for that I could help out for a few hours at their front desk. Then I've got therapy. Dr. Gill's gonna help me request accommodations for my exam in August."

"I'll drive you."

"You don't have to do that. I was gonna ride my bike."

"You can't ride that thing. The wheels are all messed up."

"*Nah*," I dismiss him with a wave. "It's fine. I've been riding it these past couple weeks, no problem. I have to pedal harder, that's all."

"Well, now you don't have to." His mouth tightens. "You could get yourself hurt."

And why does he care?

"I'm a grown woman." Barely a functioning adult, but okay, Behraz. "I'm not your responsibility."

Fletcher frowns. "Doesn't mean you're allowed to risk getting hurt."

"*Fine*," I say through a sigh. "You can drive me."

He goes upright and folds his arms across his broad chest. "Good."

My index finger wags. "But this is not gonna be an everyday thing."

CHAPTER 9:
OVERDUE FOR A GOOD WALLOW

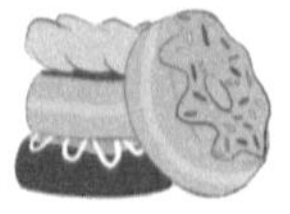

FLETCHER

DRIVING BEHRAZ AROUND EVERY DAY IS MY FAVORITE part of the day.

I could listen to her talk forever.

And to think, this brilliant woman thought she was stupid. A tragedy, really.

It's nice not to worry about initiating conversation or if I'm asking too many personal questions when she offers it up herself.

In a matter of a couple of weeks, I've learned so much about her. And I don't want to stop.

"Wait, did you not know I was Parsi?" she asked when I commented that the language she spoke with her parents on the phone was similar to what I'd heard Indi use with her family.

I didn't know. The Google search for the word gulabi had inconclusive results, spanning across the languages of Hindi, Urdu, and Farsi. And I misspelled Parsi as Farsi, confusing me further.

"Seemed rude to ask."

She clapped her hands together as we idled in traffic. "Time for a little history lesson. Parsi basically means Persian."

Oh, so she's Iranian? *I thought to myself.*

"But my ancestors fled Iran during the Islamic conquest, because we're Zoroastrians and were being persecuted."

"Oh. I'm sorry."

"Please, it was hundreds of years ago. Anyway, my ancestors basically ended up on the west coast of India and were given asylum by the then-king of Gujarat. There was a lot of assimilation, so we speak Gujarati, too, like Indi, and a lot of our culture is the same, but there are differences in religious customs and traditional food."

"That's cool."

Unlike that response, numbnuts.

"And like many other Gujarati business people during the British rule of India, Parsis found themselves in various colonies where the opportunity arose. My great-grandparents moved from Mumbai to Uganda, then my grandparents shifted to Tanzania, where my parents were born. My brother and I were born there, too."

I nodded along.

"Dad's cement business had him traveling to Oman a lot for various construction contracts, so eventually we moved there. When things were unpredictable financially, we moved to Canada. My mom's best friend from high school convinced her it was a stable place to live and for us to get a good education. But my dad kept getting contracts in Oman, and Mom didn't want to move us while we were almost done with middle and high school, so she called my Granny to come live with us in Ottawa. Oh, Granny hated the cold. My mom missed the easy life of luxury she had in Muscat. When Parvez started culinary school and I was in class 8, Mom started traveling with Dad, being away for months at a time."

"Wow. That's—"

"Sorry, word vomit."

"I think you might be the only Persian-Indian-African-Middle Eastern-Canadian I know."

It made for a hell of an accent. I loved it.

"Isn't the South Asian diaspora fun?"

I find myself totally in awe of her resilience. She's been through so many changes and experiences within such a young life, and to be pure sunshine and emanate joy despite it? She's amazing.

Today's ride home is no less exciting. It's wild to witness her go from talking about how therapy helped her realize her humor is a trauma response from a fear of acceptance in a new place to how her nanny in Tanzania used to sing her lullabies in Swahili, and how homemade rosewater is her grandmother's secret to healthy skin and asking if I want to do skincare and wallow with her on Friday because her accommodations request got denied.

"I'm guessing by your silence it's a no."

"Sorry, I spaced." I shake my head. "I'll join for the first part. I'm overdue for a good wallow, but what does skincare entail?"

"I was thinking a turmeric mask with olive and honey—"

"Sounds sticky."

"True, and the yellow might stain your skin. We can't have that, but *ooh!* We could do a mud mask with rosewater. I think I still have some multani maati, I'll just have to find it..."

She explains the ingredients and how to prep the mask as we change lanes and continue on our way home.

Friday, it is.

———

Thursday night, I put down my copy of Analeigh Sbrana's *Lore of the Wilds* when a clang follows hurried shuffles in the space outside of my bedroom. Through the crack in the door, I snoop on Behraz tucking a bottle of whiskey into the liquor cabinet before leaving with a bag slung over one shoulder. A thin layer of amber lingers in the shot glass she abandons on the counter next to the sink.

She doesn't see me, but the brief glimpse is too long, because now the image of her in one of those short dresses with tiny, delicate flowers all over them is gonna be stuck in my brain forever. She pre-gamed. She obviously had plans. Plans that didn't include me.

And why would they include you? You don't even like having plans. You'd cancel plans if you even had them. Though I like anything that has to do with her. I retrace her steps, inhaling the incredible scent of roses she's left behind, trying not to think about who she has plans with.

Yikes. I need to go cool off before I start feeling jealous of someone who possibly doesn't exist. But what if they *do* exist?

I jog back to my room and change into a pair of swimming shorts, grabbing a beach towel from the linen closet before taking the elevator to the rooftop.

The air is cool against my bare skin, but the pool is supposed to be heated, so I suffer the goosebumps from the shirtless walk from the lounge chair to the water. I clamp my eyes shut while taking a dunk, and sigh loudly when returning to the surface, swiping the damp hair back from my face and stripping my beard of excess water. Sitting up on the edge of the pool, I keep my legs in the water. The view is nice from up here. Lit up Gothic-style church steeples and parliament buildings line the dark sky alongside more modern skyscrapers and glassy condo buildings like mine. My arms prop behind me while searching for any sort of star, but it's no use. There's too much light pollution. After a few minutes, my gaze returns to the water. I freeze. I'm not alone.

The dark figure at the corner of the pool moves to an underwater light, only her head visible in the deeper end. Every muscle in my body tenses tighter and tighter as Behraz wades closer, exposing more and more of her body above the surface of the water.

Her hair is slicked back from being wet. Oh, God. She's wet all over, dripping with the saltwater from the pool. Droplets hang from her lips, crown her defined collarbone, and hug her shoulders. Only two strings sit tied around her slender neck, her full chest bobbing below the water line.

Don't stare. Don't stare at her tits.

"Hi," she starts.

"Hi," I whisper back.

My nipples shrink, tightening to the point of pain. I release the edge to dip into the water, bending my knees to submerge my chest. The heat of the pool feels cool against the flush rising on my skin.

She turns to walk backward to the stairs, revealing even more of her body. "I got sick of studying. Thought I could clear my head with a swim."

"Same." My head shakes a denial. "I mean, I came to clear my head, too."

But my brain is filled with thoughts of you, I want to say. And it doesn't seem to want to be free of them. I think my heart might explode.

Behraz stands on the bottom step and looks up, showing me her perfect chest and the curve of her bare waist. "Isn't it crazy?"

Yeah, whoa. This *is* crazy. She looks...phenomenal. My cock pulses.

Shh. Go away. Let me have this.

"What's...crazy?"

"How insignificant we are compared to" —she waves a hand in a semi-circle over her head— "all of this."

"Uh-huh."

You're a pervert. Stop. Staring. At. Her. Nipples. But they're—

"Fletcher?"

"Yeah?"

"They're pierced."

I clench my eyes closed. "I—"

I'm pretty sure this pool water is boiling me alive. She sits and reclines on her elbows on the step behind her, tossing her head back to laugh. The subtle movement sends trickles of water down her breasts and returns them to the pool. "It's okay to look. I know you're otherwise a gentleman."

A gentleman who wants to untie your top with his teeth, strip it away, and suck on your tits until they're dry. A gentleman who wants your pretty mouth on every inch of my skin.

"Right." I flatten my arms over the cement edge of the pool in an attempt to appear relaxed.

"Hey, Fletcher?"

"Mmm?"

She chews on the inside of her cheek, leaving a dimple. "I know I said I didn't want you to, but thanks for driving me to work and around town."

"Of course."

Her teeth sink into her lower lip next. I suddenly and desperately want to be her teeth at this moment. Christ, Fletch. You sound deranged.

"And I know I talk a lot, so thanks for listening, too. It makes me feel less alone."

Her eyes lock onto mine, and I can't help the grin splitting my reddened face.

"Anytime."

CHAPTER 10:
FLETCHER DONOVAN IS A SLUT

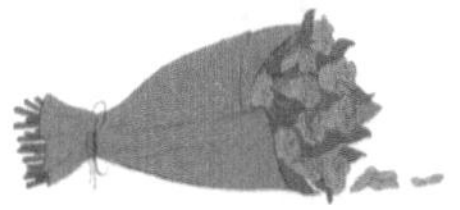

BEHRAZ

I MIGHT BE DYING.

Last night, Fletcher Donovan, God amongst men, saw me in the tiniest bathing suit I own. And I'm pretty sure I saw...all of him. Pecs, abs, and an impossible-to-ignore outline of a massive dick. Which is impressive considering water typically causes shrinkage. My mind. It's permanently in the gutter.

It doesn't help that he's always around, being kind and caring and blushing up a storm. On top of that, the air conditioning in the apartment is going haywire. My bedroom is no colder than a sauna, and sitting in the living area requires multiple layers.

I throw on grey sweats and an old tee. It's from a small gift shop in Montreal from a few years ago. Indi took me and her sister on a quick girls' trip when Landon was a client and got us club seating for a game. One of the best weekends of my life. I peek out the door.

Oh, good. He's not here. Now I can finally study. He's so distracting. Really, really distracting. And how am I supposed to pay attention when he's everywhere, walking around the apartment with his handsome face stuck in a book?

Stack of flashcards in hand, I tuck the exam prep manual under an arm and wrap myself in the one salmon pink blanket I managed to finish while in my finger-knitting phase.

The blanket burrito falls apart when I sit on the couch and extend my legs. I adjust it under my ass and pull it over my shoulders, but lose grip of the flashcards. They explode across the space like confetti.

"Perfect. Well done, Bea," I deadpan. I'll collect those later. First, a review. I stare at the Comprehensive Bar Exam Preparation Manual. So much for studying. The cover of this cursed exam prep manual is the exact same color as Fletcher's perfect, rich, thick, auburn hair. Hair that I want to run my hands through. Give a good yank while I ride his face. Fuck, I am way too horny to be studying right now. Maybe I should go rub one out. No. What if he comes home and catches you? Bad idea. I set a timer on my phone for thirty minutes. Alright, let's try this Pomodoro method business.

Taking a deep breath, I start to read, but the words don't make any sense. Focus, Bea, focus. Focus, focus, focus. The door lock clicks. My roommate steps through, kicking off his shoes before walking to the kitchen and removing his over-the-ear headphones. I gape at his outfit.

Fletcher Donovan is a slut. A slutty slut slut-slut.

A cropped Ottawa Regents shirt with the sleeves cut off exposes his bulky arms and toned abs. Black shorts with a *very* short inseam cut across his muscular thighs and highlight the slutty trail of dark red hair traveling downward from his belly button. He turns to grab a glass from the cupboard, round, juicy ass on display. Jeez, did he go out like that?

Fletcher fills the glass and rounds the counter, bringing it to his lips before noticing my presence. He stills, pushing a hand through his mussed hair and turning a particular shade of crimson that has me crossing my legs and curling my toes. Unbelievable. The man makes me wet because he blushes.

"Hey," he says through a breath.

"Hey," I reply, moving my eyes across the open page. The words make even less sense now.

"Your book's upside down."

Hey, Earth? How about you swallow me whole?

I hide the flush flaming my face with the manual. "That's 'cause I'm stupid."

"You're not stupid, Behraz."

Another exhale hisses through my teeth. "I really suck at studying. I took a practice exam this morning. It was worse than my last attempt."

"Shit."

"I'm trying all the different tips and methods to stay organized, but" —my hands show the mess of flashcards scattered across the sofa, coffee table, and floor— "surprise, surprise. I'm failing spectacularly."

Fletcher walks over and sits on the cushion by my feet. "Can I help?"

You can help by not being a little slut and wearing slutty little outfits around the apartment. That'd be a great help.

"You're already helping me so much. I'm living here rent-free; you chauffeur me around to work and therapy."

"So?"

"I don't know." I tilt my head back to rest on the arm of the couch. "I'm starting to think I'm unhelpable."

"Also not true." He takes a generous gulp of water, halving the amount in the glass. Watching his throat wobble makes my thighs clench tighter. "My little sister, Harper." Fletcher burps quietly through a fist. "Excuse me. She has ADHD, too."

"Really?"

"Yeah, she got diagnosed right after she graduated from uni." His glass empties with the next gulp. He sets it down and wipes a line of sweat from his freckled forehead. "She's the smartest of us, and we didn't really understand how she got through all the years of studying without any trouble, but she struggled. We didn't see it, because she was working hard."

"Yeah."

"But I guess working was a completely different structure from school. And moving across the country was a big change. She got support through her job. I spent that summer with her, doing some research and figuring out what worked."

"You'd do that for me, too?"

"Whatever I can." His shoulders tense and drop. "I'm pretty useless otherwise."

My heart rips in two. Is that what he thinks of himself? "You're joking, right?" I sit up and scoot forward until my feet touch the floor. "You're literally saving my ass on the daily."

"Pretty sure you saved my ass, too."

"After I nearly killed you."

"*Ha*, true." His laugh. What a sound. One of his thumbs picks at his lips. "Maybe we're saving each other, Behraz."

It's freezing in here, and I'm melting.

"Maybe."

"Are...are we still on for wallowing and skincare tonight?" He rises from the couch, bringing his crotch to my line of sight. Stop looking, Bea. You're a creep. But his dick is unavoidable. How it's being withheld in those tiny shorts is a true mystery. "Because believe it or not, I'm getting old. I think I saw a wrinkle in the mirror this morning."

I deny him with a roll of my eyes. "You do *not* have wrinkles, and you're *not* old."

"I'm almost thirty," he argues.

"So am I."

"No way."

"I am. I'm twenty-seven."

"I'm twenty-eight."

I know. Because I'm a stalker who knows how to use the internet, and you're the public figure I've had an enormous crush on for about six years.

"Alright, old man," I tease. "Skincare tonight. I'll prep the mud mask."

I'll never get tired of his sweet smiles. They're so rare and subtle. Like they're just for me.

"Sounds like a plan."

———

Ambient electric guitars play over the speaker in the living room as we recline on the couch. Cool slices of cucumber cover our eyes.

"I cand murr by fayshe," Fletcher mumbles.

I can't either but reply through tight lips. "Dash how you know ish working."

He exhales through his nose. "Hurr mush lurrngurr?"

The timer goes off, and I tap his arm, signaling we can go wash our faces.

A few minutes later, we emerge from our respective washrooms.

"I think it worked." Fletcher pats his face. "I look younger already."

"Has anyone ever called you dramatic?"

A guilty smile stretches his clean skin. "Never."

"Also, that was only skincare, step one." I pat a spot on the sofa cushion next to me. "Tilt your head back." He obeys. I do like a man who listens.

"Step two is toner. Homemade rosewater is my favorite." The small spray bottle swishes with the liquid inside. "Eyes closed." I spritz five times and do the same to myself. "Now we let it dry."

"This is so involved," he concludes. "I had no idea."

"Last is a moisturizer. Extra thick since it's gonna be overnight, mixed in with a nighttime serum for hydration." I offer the heavy cream and a few drops of serum in his palm, demonstrating how to mix and apply it.

"Did I do it right?" Fletcher tilts his head left and right to show me. I nod. "Cool."

I mirror the action. "How about me?"

"Just" —he taps a spot on his cheek— "here, can I?"

My throat tightens. "Yeah."

I almost lose control of my breathing when his thumb swipes over the line of my jaw to rub a missed spot of moisturizer in.

His phone interrupts with a buzz, breaking the tension. "Alright, food's here." Fletcher gets up and moves toward the front door.

"What did you order?"

"Poutine. Is that okay?"

I cross my legs beneath me on the couch, motioning for him to hand it over. "Hell, yes. It's my favorite."

He pulls his lips into his mouth while removing the baskets of cheesy, gravy-covered fries from their foil sleeves. "I know."

My eyebrows lift. "You do?"

"I noticed you eating it that day when I caught you crying. And half a dozen other times when you were upset. I figured it was a comfort food."

"It is." I pause to thank him with a smile. "Thanks, Fletcher."

"Anytime." He passes me a fork and a napkin before settling himself into the couch, too. "So, when do we wallow?"

"You know, it's weird," I say between gooey, delicious bites. "I don't really feel like wallowing anymore."

CHAPTER 11:
I'VE NEVER BEEN ON A DATE BEFORE

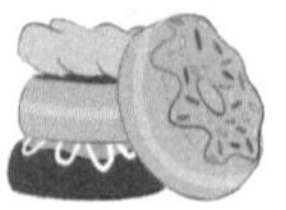

FLETCHER

I MUNCH ON SOME POPCORN WHILE WAITING FOR Antiques Roadshow to return to the screen.

It's the closest I'll get to betting while the guys are away.

Behraz throws open her door and gives me a thumbs up. "Brown noise with the Pomodoro method helped. I got all the flashcards right!"

"Nice." She joins me on the couch. My heart rate picks up. "Taking a break?"

"Just ten minutes or so." A fistful of popcorn disappears from my bowl and into her mouth. "Whatcha watching?"

"Antiques Roadshow."

"Wow," she says through a crunch, "you really are a nerd."

"I know. But I like what I like."

An older woman appears on screen, seated with the appraiser at a table. *"Alright, Betty. What do you have for us today?"*

"So this is a family heirloom that I received when my grandmother died. I've always been told it's an emerald pendant on a gold chain, and it was gifted to her on her first date with my grandfather."

Behraz snorts. "Dating is so different now." She steals another handful of popcorn, and I slyly leave the bowl on her lap. "I swear I couldn't pay someone to take me on a date."

"Sorry? *You've* never been on a date?" I mean, *I've* never been on a date, but I'm a pathetic loser. Behraz, though? She's everything. I'd date her so hard.

"No need to rub it in."

"I'm not, I'm just surprised."

"I don't know. I've been bought drinks or hooked up with people—"

My heart plops to my stomach and swirls around.

"But you know, never a date-date. No one's ever asked to take me out for dinner, or brought me flowers, or anything like that. It's kinda sad being perpetually single, but then again...maybe it's for the best. I could never keep up with all the expectations of any relationships and at least this way I didn't hurt anyone but myself."

What a goddamn shame. She deserves a room full of flowers. Endless meals she doesn't have to pay for. Someone to wait on her, hand and foot. Someone to worship her. I wish it could be me.

"It's not much solace, but I've never been on a date before either."

"Seriously?"

Social anxiety isn't really conducive to flirting.

"I'm not good in social situations most of the time. It makes me so anxious to go to a crowded place and make small talk. Especially with wo-men." My shoulders tense, then drop. "It never seems right, always forced and like...like they want something from me that I can't give them. And also there's fear that whatever I have to offer, they're not interested." I'm spouting nonsensical rambles instead of being able to admit that she's the only woman I've wanted since I was twenty-two. "Sorry, I have no idea what I'm saying."

"No, I get it," she says, tilting her head in my direction. "And I hate to break it to you, but...I'm a woman, and you talk to me."

"That's different." 'Cause I'm obsessed with you in an unhealthy way. And you still make me nervous as hell. "It's easy with you," I admit, and it feels like a weight dropped from my shoulders. You're all I want.

A light gleams in Behraz's eyes. "Maybe *we* should go on a date."

My face heats. "What?"

"Not romantically, just...as friends. It's the least I can do." She hands over the empty bowl of popcorn. "You let me stay here, drive me around. At least this way, you get something out of me being here, too."

Her being here is everything to me.

Bea nods in confirmation to herself. "Then, when you go on a real date, you'll know what to do."

A real date? What makes her think I wanna go on a date with anyone else but her? And why can't I just say that?

Her phone rings out, the timer signaling her break is over. "Okay, back to studying."

"See ya."

"Don't for a second think you're off the hook, Mister." She waves a finger at me. "I'll be back in thirty minutes. Think of some date ideas and we'll discuss."

Before I can protest, her bedroom door slams shut.

Fuck me, I'm gonna be practice-dating Behraz Irani.

———

"Fletcher?" Behraz calls from across the apartment a couple of hours later. "Could you come in here?"

I approach her bedroom door, my steps quiet and tentative. I point. "In there? In your bedroom?"

"Yes, you silly goose. Sit right here." She pats a spot on her bed next to where she sits against the headboard. "I need help with this crossword. I'm trying to be good and finish."

Oh, my mind is filthy. Incorrigible.

"C'mon, hurry up," Behraz demands. "What, have you never sat on a girl's bed before?"

I've never sat on a girl's bed before. At least, not a girl who wasn't my sister.

"Oh, my God. You've never sat on a girl's bed before."

There's a warmth crawling up my chest, ready to turn into an embarrassing blush. Goddamnit.

"I'm so sorry, Fletcher. That was rude of me."

"It's fine," I try to shrug it off with humor. "I've had opportunities, I'll have you know, but I'll only sit on a girl's bed when I'm good and ready."

There's an awkward lull while Bea stares into the air above her head, wondering what the fuck I'm talking about.

"Are...you ready now?"

"Right, yes. I'm ready." I lower to the mattress, folding one leg underneath the opposite knee, leaving one foot on the ground. "What's the clue?"

"Four-letter word. Third letter, T. Feed the kitty." She drops the pen and throws her arms up. "All the answers I have are dirty and don't fit."

That'd be me, too, but this one I actually know.

"Ante."

"A-n-t-i?"

"E instead of i. It's a poker term."

"Kitty is a poker term?"

I lift my palms in surrender. "I don't make the rules."

"I trust you." She fills out the squares and thinks about the word perpendicular to it. There are only a couple of letters missing. "Cafeteria shout, cafeteria shout." The end of her pen taps against her lips. "Oh! Food fight!"

"Nicely done."

She jumps to her knees, punching the air in victory. "Woo hoo! I did it, I did it."

All the bouncing is doing horribly embarrassing things to my groin. I gotta get out of here. I scramble to my feet and head towards the open door.

"Hey, get back here. Where are your date ideas?"

I tap my temple with my finger. "All up here."

"Nope, not good enough." She slides off the bed. "Hold on." Behraz steps into the walk-in closet and roots around in a box, then emerges with a handful of popsicle sticks and a glass Mason jar.

"What's this?"

"To write down the ideas." Each wooden stick gets numbered, and she hands me a few. "Then we put them in this jar, and whenever we need an idea, we'll pick one and do it."

"We're going on more than one date?"

"I'll treat you real nice," she says through a Southern drawl, pumping her eyebrows.

I cover my mouth with a hand, but the blush spreads too far above my cheeks.

"Practice makes perfect, Fletcher. It'll be fun."

"Okay, but I have one condition."

"*Ooh*, I live for a negotiation. Let's hear it."

"We only go on a date if you finish your material for the day."

"Tough guy, eh?" She puts up fists and fakes boxing like Curly from the Three Stooges before breaking out into a spectacularly bright smile. "Deal."

CHAPTER 12:
I'M NO BETTER THAN A MAN

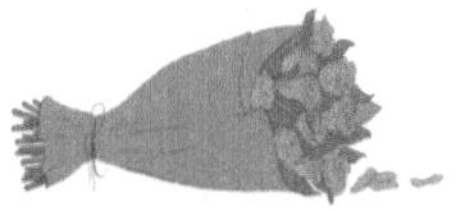

BEHRAZ

I'M DEFINITELY STUPID.

Because why else would I ask my crush and roommate to go on multiple fake dates with me while I pretend they're not real dates? Oh, I'm so screwed. Or rather, *not* screwed by Fletcher Donovan. Only screwed by myself and my small collection of sex toys.

I definitely *need* to go on a date with Fletcher. Just to see how it is. Maybe it'll suck, and then I put this impossible fantasy to bed once and for all. Or maybe he'll throw me in a bed, once and for all. No! This is for him. You're helping *him* out. He's helped you, now you help him.

I check my nose in the mirror. "It hasn't grown, so I'm not lying to myself or anything," I say quietly, turning off the washroom fan. I pop my lips to make sure the rosy-pink stain doesn't spread, adjusting my bra one last time to make sure the girls are secure. "Here we go."

Fletcher gets to his feet from his seat on the sofa, face painted with shock.

"Well, look at you all cleaned up," I state, checking out the denim button-up with rolled sleeves he paired with tan chino shorts. It's a significant step up from the usual sweats and tees, and almost as slutty as those injurious-to-my-health crop tops. "Ready for our date?"

He clears his throat. "Yeah." But he doesn't move.

"Fletcher?"

"Oh, right." A bouquet of peonies wrapped in burlap and tied with twine is handed over. "These are for you."

"My first flowers from a boy," I gush. My stomach does a happy dance. This smile is not going to go away anytime soon. "Thank you."

He still doesn't move. "You look…"

God, he's so sweet. I smooth a hand over the belly of this blush pink milkmaid dress, then puff the sleeves. "This dress is cute, right?"

"I was gonna say gorgeous."

Yeah, this smile isn't going anywhere.

"See?" I wink, eliciting a rampant blush from him. "You're doing an amazing job on this date already. Now let's go."

I practically float to the Rideau Canal.

Fletcher picks a shady spot and lays a classic gingham blanket down, placing the basket in the middle.

I slip off my sandals and sit, shoving my sunglasses to the top of my head. "It's beautiful today."

"Yeah, it's really beautiful," he echoes.

When I glance over, he's looking at me.

"That was smooth, Casanova." My sunglasses return to hide my eyes.

Fletcher kneels to unpack our dinner, arranging a wooden tray with grapes, sliced cheese squares, and some fancy water crackers. It gets placed between us before he retrieves two glasses and a can from the woven basket. "It's Leinenkugel's Summer Shandy."

"Is that a beer?"

"If beer were a lemonade."

"Sounds delicious."

A thin layer of foam builds in both cups as he pours. We clink the glasses together and take a sip. He's right. It's citrusy and crisp, bubbly the whole way down my throat, and warms my belly. Though that could be the company, too. I nibble on a cracker paired with a spreadable goat cheese, motioning to the path adjacent to the canal. "Good people watching, too. Check out those two." I vaguely point to a couple having an intense discussion and imitate a Newfoundland accent. "This is the last time, Fred. If you leave your filthy drars outside the laundry basket *one more time*, I'm gonna lose it!"

Fletcher chokes on his grape. I keep going.

"Or those bros." Two meaty, sweaty joggers speed along, passing the arguing couple. I lower my voice an octave and put on a California surfer accent. "Nah, man. I'm telling you, the whey isolate protein powder is the way to go. It's expensive and gives you diarrhea, but it's the only way to effectively bulk up without shrinking your balls down to the size of peas."

My roommate snickers, his shoulders shaking as he smiles. I can't stop now.

Two young women wearing oversized Carleton University tees over bike shorts take turns whispering to one another and giggling.

I lift my pitch, higher than my normal tone. "He asked me if I liked it, *heeheehee*! And...Oh, my god, what did you say? I told him I couldn't feel it! *Heeheehee*, that small? Oh no! Then he cried! *Heeheehee*. I had to leave!"

"Bea," Fletcher chides through a chuckle. "*Jesus.*"

"Hey, that's the first time you called me that." I nudge with an elbow. "I like it."

He takes out a container of cucumber sandwiches and hands me one half. I try it before skewering a ball of fresh mozzarella, tomato, and a leaf of basil with a toothpick.

"You went all out with this spread. It's so classy."

"It's from the store. I can't cook nearly as well as you do."

"Stop, you're such a flirt." I shake my head at him. "But go on." A group of four beautiful women on rollerblades laugh as they pass. "*Whew.*" I fan myself. "I'm no better than a man."

"What do you mean?"

"They're hot."

"If you say so," he adds, opening another can of beer and refreshing our drinks.

"You don't think so?"

"Not really. But you're allowed to be attracted to whoever you want."

"It doesn't make you uncomfortable?"

"What doesn't?"

"That I'm attracted to women, too?"

"Is it supposed to? It's who you are, right?"

"Yeah. It is."

Easy as that. Not sure any man has accepted it so quickly, at least not without suggesting a three-way. Then again, I've never really hung out with decent men.

My hand drops next to his on the blanket, centimeters away from touching.

He nurses the rest of his beer while watching two boys toss a lacrosse ball back and forth. The younger one misses, and the ball goes into the water. "*Aw, come on, Sam!*" The older one scolds and goes on a rant. *"You coulda caught that!"*

"What a dick," Fletcher mumbles. "Sounds like my brother."

I hiss. "Sorry."

"Not your fault. Parker's been angry for a long time."

"Why is that?"

"Park was the hockey all-star." He keeps his sunglasses on, despite the setting sun. "Got drafted to Winnipeg right out of high school, got some decent play time for a rookie, too. But he got into a car accident in the middle of his second season. He'd been drinking and lost control over a patch of black ice. Smashed right into a lamppost and shattered his left knee. He was only nineteen, so they did surgery, months of physical therapy, but it always gave him trouble."

"That really sucks."

Fletcher nods with a sniffle. "They ended his contract because he couldn't play without injuring himself. He came home and started coaching. My dad was livid. He thought he'd gotten a free ticket to finally get out of Summerside. Instead, Parker pushed me into it, hoping for a better outcome. I made it farther, I suppose, but it's still not good enough."

"God, Fletcher."

"I shouldn't complain. It's a job."

"What would you do if you didn't play?"

"No idea. It's the only thing I'm good at."

"That's not true." An ache settles into my chest, and I close the small space between our hands. Our pinkies nearly touch. "You're good at having a kind, generous heart. You're good at listening, like, *really* listening. You're good at being dependable. And honestly," I pause to breathe, afraid I'll forget to, "all of those things are way more important than being good at hockey."

CHAPTER 13:
BEHRAZ IRANI HELD MY HAND

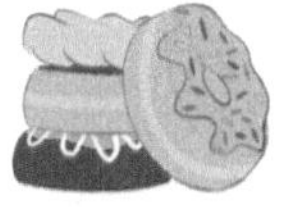

FLETCHER

WHEN HER HAND DROPS TO THE BLANKET, OUR PINKIES overlap.

She straightens with a jolt, and my whole body seizes. Neither of us move from the position for a few moments. And then she does. Just her little finger. Not away. No. It shifts. Slow, delicate strokes. Testing. And that gentle touch? It feels stronger, burns hotter than the blazing sun before us. I want to grip that feeling, hold that tiny piece of her so close it sears into my soul and never let go.

Maybe she pities me after hearing my sob story, but I don't care. If she wants to touch me, she sure as shit gets to.

"We should head back before it gets dark and the mosquitoes come to feast."

I nod in agreement and pack up the food, then wait for her to stand before folding the blanket and tucking it into the basket.

The walk home is wordless. I stay on the streetside. Our hands brush every time they sway, like pendulums that keep missing each other.

Then, some asshole on an electric scooter comes flying down the sidewalk, almost knocking into Behraz. I pull her out of the way, but it's too late. Her pretty pink dress is covered with a grimy splatter of mud.

"Hey!" I scream after him, but he doesn't stop.

"It's okay, I'm fine." She tugs at my hand. "We're almost home."

I glare over my shoulder, but Bea holds tight, lacing our fingers together and replacing my anger with nervous tension. And our hands stay like that, locked together, until we get to the door of our apartment. I don't want to, but when Bea's hand relaxes, I let go.

"I'm gonna go get cleaned up," she announces.

"Okay."

Her bedroom door snaps shut, and I run to mine, launching myself onto the bed like an overexcited child. I roll to my back, kicking the mattress and covering my face with my palms.

Behraz Irani held my hand.

I pat my chest, calming myself through deep breaths, but it's no use. My heart will never recover from this. My phone vibrates, cutting the swoonfest short. It's a FaceTime call from Piper. I answer. My niece, Lila's face appears on the screen.

"Hiya!"

"Hey, Lila! What's up?"

"Uncle Fletcher," she intones. "It's my birthday!"

"I know, sweet girl. That's why I called this morning. Your mom let you stay up late for your birthday, huh? Big 1-0!"

"It's only 8 p.m. I'm not a baby anymore."

"Oops, sorry. You're still a baby to me."

"Uncle Fletcher, *stopppp*."

"Okay, okay."

"And where's my birthday present?"

"*Hmmm*." I tap my forefinger to my chin. "It shoulda been there already."

"I didn't get it."

"*Oooh*. I think I know what happened. Do me a favor and give the phone to your mom."

"Okay, one sec."

The kid's getting too big. I still remember holding her at the hospital.

My oldest sister takes control of the phone. "Hi, Fletcher."

"Hey, Pipe. How's the party?"

"I've got seven ten-year-olds, five eight-year-olds, and three six-year-olds running the house into the ground. How do you think it's going?"

"Sounds like Christmas at the Donovans."

"Worse, I'd say."

I narrow my eyes at her. "I see. Now, what'd ya do with the box I sent last week?"

She sighs. "It's too much, Fletcher."

"Oh, come on, she's ten now. And it's only a Nintendo Switch. I don't get to spoil them as much as I want."

"Fine. But take it easy at Christmas this year. I can't have the kids expecting bigger and more expensive gifts every year."

"Yeah, yeah. Can you give it to her now? I wanna see if she likes it or not."

Lila returns to the screen. "Mommy said she'll be back in a sec."

Her face lights up when she's handed the box, and a giddy shriek sounds out when she opens it.

"You like it?"

"Thank you, thank you, thank you!" She hugs the phone, and my heart grows.

"I'm sorry I missed the party."

"Come visit soon, okay? I wanna go on the jet skis like we did last summer."

"You got it, kiddo. Have fun."

"Bye, Uncle Fletcher!"

We wave to each other before she ends the call.

I lie back on the pillow and sigh out again, glancing at my hand and tracing the space between each finger, memorizing how Behraz's fingers felt between them.

A crash follows a loud clang. What was that?

"Fletcher?" her voice calls weakly.

Oh, no.

CHAPTER 14:
BRUISED, NAKED AND TANGLED

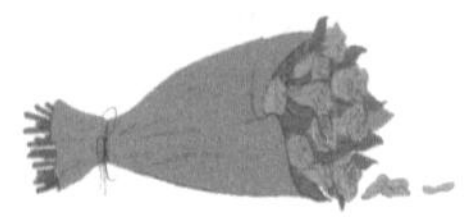

BEHRAZ

LEAVE IT TO ME TO RUIN A PRACTICALLY PERFECT DATE.

Fletcher held my hand. I got splattered with sludge, but still. He held my hand. And it made me so nervous, my stomach couldn't handle it. I almost soil myself before booking it to the washroom and nearly destroy the toilet.

A steamy shower does wash away the grime and relaxes me a bit, but when I turn off the water and slide open the glass, this particular shit smells so awful, I need to close the toilet lid. My two left feet slip when I lean over to do so, and I fall right out of the tub. In a split second, one knee lands on the shower door's track, the other knee hitting the drying mat as my shoulder slams into the glass edge of the shower panel. My elbow hits the toilet seat while trying to reach for anything that will stabilize me. Instead, what I grab is the flush handle, and the toilet water swirls down what's left of my dignity as my head slaps against the back wall, dangerously close to the toilet brush handle sticking out of its holder.

That's gonna leave a mark.

I'm bruised, naked, and tangled, but manage to pull the towel from the bar across the shower door. I wait a few minutes to stand on my own, but ultimately give up. There's no way he didn't hear that. "Fletcher?"

A knock raps on the door. "You okay?"

"Not exactly."

"Are you hurt?"

"Only my dignity. And other things."

"Is it okay if I unlock it?"

"Yes. No, wait!" I warn. "I'm not wearing anything. Keep your eyes closed."

The door swings open, and Fletcher blindly walks in with his arms extended in front of him, feeling out the air. "How am I supposed to help you if I can't see you?" He peeks through one eye at my curled form by the toilet.

I clutch the corner of the terry cloth, hoping it covers enough of me.

"Oh, Bea."

Somehow, he simultaneously wraps me in the towel and picks me up until I'm sitting on the toilet lid. I rub the sore spot on my forehead.

Fletcher inspects it with a grimace. "That might leave a bump."

My hands tighten around the overlapping flaps of the towel wrapped around my chest.

His throat swallows audibly. "Do you...do you have any clothes in here?"

"There's a shirt on the back of the door."

He grabs it and slips it over my head without looking, helping my arms through the sleeves.

Then he blinks three times. "That's my jersey."

"Yeah."

Don't make a big deal of it. He'll think you're a weirdo. But you *are* a weirdo.

"Do you mind? I need to put on...something under this."

Flustered and red, he exits the washroom.

I slip on a pair of soft pajama shorts and hang up the towel, using the sink for support before reopening the door.

Fletcher waits at the foot of my bed. "You wear my jersey?"

"Why the face? I happen to think I look pretty good in it, don't you?" I hobble and pivot on the leg that hurts less, turning to show him the back. "Do you like it?"

"More than I should."

"What does that mean?"

Maybe *I* have a concussion.

"Nothing." He rubs the back of his neck. "You should probably take it easy."

"*Um*, yeah, probably."

"Okay, well. Good night."
"Good night." My ass drops to the mattress.
Well, that was anticlimactic.

———

I laze in bed and replay the end of the evening a dozen times early the next morning before grabbing my phone.

ME

I had a great time last night

DREAMBOAT

I did too

ME

It was looking dicey for a second with the washroom snafu

ME

Thanks for rescuing me

I send him a GIF of Olive Oyl swooning with the caption, "*My hero!*"

ME

Congrats on a successful first date for both of us

A soft ding peals out beyond my door. Is he in the living room? I slink down from the mattress and tiptoe to the door, pressing an ear to it. No movement. Seems like the coast is clear. The door opens with a creak. Fletch sits on the couch facing my bedroom door.

"Oh, morning."
"Morning."
My cautious steps quicken as I near him, overeager to spill my heart out, but he beats me to it.
"I have to tell you something."

Heart thumping in my throat, I murmur, "Yeah?"

"Last night...holding your hand. It felt..."

"...Right?" I finish the sentence for him, hoping he agrees and that I didn't imagine it all.

He puffs out a breath, relieved. "Yeah, it felt right. It felt safe."

I pinch back a smile. "It felt like that for me, too."

Fletcher surges with a blush, and I'm on top of the world.

"So, I know it's against the date idea jar rules," I begin, "but if I finish my practice questions today, wanna go wildflower picking?"

"Can we hold hands again? F-for practice."

"Sure, Fletcher. We can practice."

If Fletcher Donovan asked me to sleep on the highway, I'd agree with a smile. This silly, bashful man is going to ruin me.

CHAPTER 15:
WHAT ABOUT THE HAND HOLDING?

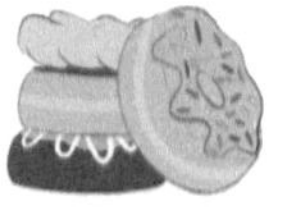

FLETCHER

"IT SAYS HERE IT'S ILLEGAL IN ONTARIO TO PLUCK wildflowers from where they naturally grow."

"Damn it," Bea snaps. "Now what?"

"We could choose another idea."

"Wait—I've got it!" She hustles to the foyer and shoves her feet into slip-on sneakers. "Come on, come on."

"Where are we going?"

"Just drive, I'll show you." We race down the hallway and into the pickup. "Take Rideau toward 99." She giggles, the mischievous, childlike glee making her cheeks go rosy. For the next ten minutes, I'm too busy admiring her to notice we arrive at a familiar neighborhood. "Okay, stop here."

The hypnosis clears. I squint and look up through the passenger window. "What are we doing at Gabe and Wade's?"

"You'll see in a second," she assures. Once we park, Bea leads me by the hand to the security desk. If my hand is in hers, I'd follow her anywhere.

She addresses the guard at the desk with a honeyed lilt. "Hi there, *Stephen*. How's it going?"

Stephen's response is delayed while he side-eyes her. "I'm doing well, and you?"

"I'm good, I'm good." She claps a hand to the desktop. "I have a *little* problem, and I know you can help me out."

"How so?"

"Yes! You see, my friends, Gabe Finch and Wade Boehner live in the penthouse here. And I'm supposed to water their plants while they're vacationing in Florida, but—" she facepalms— "Gabe forgot to leave me a key card."

"I see."

"Their plants are so precious to them, and it's been so sunny lately, I don't want the ones on the rooftop to dry out. If you could let me and my friend here up to their penthouse—"

"Do you have ID?"

She pulls it from the small wallet stuffed in her purse. "I'm on the list. So's Fletcher" —her thumb points to me— "he's friends with Gabe and Wade, too. In fact, he and Wade play hockey together."

Stephen is still skeptical, switching his gaze between me and Behraz. "Which hockey team?"

"Ottawa's team. The Regents."

"Your ID, sir?"

The keyboard clicks as he searches our names on their safe-to-enter list. "You can go up."

"See? I told you."

"Follow me." Stephen lets us through the security turnstile and guides us to the elevators.

After a silent ride to the top floor, he uses a master key to open the penthouse.

"Thank you, Stephen!" Behraz sings, waving him off at the elevator. She then turns to me. "Flower picking time."

I'm astounded by how easy it was for her to convince him to let us up. Behraz could charm the pants off just about anyone, while I'm about as exciting and charming as a cabbage.

"Over here, Fletcher!" Big swooping motions beckon me to the outdoor space. I haven't been here for a while. Or maybe not this section.

Barefoot, she circles the large, raised beds that create a square perimeter around the fire pit and patio seating. Flowers in every color, shape, and height grow from them amongst tall grasses. Bea pokes around in a storage container and pulls out pruning shears and a pair of small scissors. "Here." She hands me the scissors. "How about you make me a bouquet, and I make you one?"

I agree. "What about the hand holding?"

She laughs, and it's the most glorious sound. "That happens *after* we pick flowers and make bouquets."

Three flowers come together in my grip. "Does this count as a bouquet?"

"It's been, like, two minutes."

I reek of impatience and desperation, and I don't care if she knows it. I want to hold her hand, as quickly and for as long as possible. I choose flowers that remind me of her. They're various shades of pink: the rosiness of her cheeks, her cherry blossom lips. "Alright, I think I'm done." I present the bouquet to her from behind my back. "What do you think?"

"How cute! I love them." Behraz hugs them to her chest. "Thank you."

"You're welcome."

"And here are yours," she offers.

It's a much better-looking bunch than mine. "Gorgeous."

For a second, she has me going, thinking she's walking toward me, but she backpedals and returns with a long hose. "We do have to water these, though. Gabe would be so sad if they didn't make it through July."

We alternate soaking the planters and each other's feet. The wind *accidentally* carried the spray when Behraz had control of the hose more than a few times.

"Okay, that's enough," I conclude. She squeals in delight as I wrangle the hose and spray nozzle from her grasp. "Can I hold your hand now?"

"Since you asked so nicely..." Her eyes glint with mischief. "Yes."

"Finally," I whisper. She holds them in front of her, and both sets of my fingers land on her wrists, savoring the climb up her palm and pushing between the gaps until they interlock. And all's right with the world.

"Happy now?" Behraz lifts her chin to glance up at me.

"Yes, very. I've never held anyone's hand like this."

"What?" she says through a giggle.

"I haven't."

A smirk follows the roll of her eyes. "Next, you'll say that you've never been kissed."

There's a lull. It breaks with her gasp. "I haven't," I admit.

Bea's mouth, the pretty thing, drops open cartoonishly, and it's the closest I've ever gotten to stealing a kiss.

"You've never been kissed? What about...?" She doesn't finish the question before I deny with a shake of my head. Because I know what she means to ask, and it's true.

Yep. I, Fletcher Donovan, am a virgin.

"A virgin," she echoes as if responding to my inner thought.

I fixate on our twined hands. My thumb rubs against a small stretch of flesh where her left hand's third finger meets the knuckle. "I'm pathetic, I know."

"You're not pathetic," Bea argues. "I'm just a slut."

"Don't say that."

Her grasp on my hands deepens. "I'm joking, but I'm kinda not. I know who I am, in this part of my life anyway. I know what I like and who I've been with, and I'm not ashamed of it. You shouldn't be ashamed of not being with anyone, either."

I return a slow series of silent nods.

"I'm not good at a lot of things, but...I can teach you how. If you want."

If I want? I want nothing and no one but her. If only she knew how badly and for how long. "Teach me?" If I haven't turned into a tomato already, I'm about to.

"Though there's one tiny little problem that would make it a little tricky." Our clasped hands swing between us. "The thing is, Fletcher..."

She sucks in a long breath and releases it through her nose.

"I've got the hugest crush on you."

Timeout. Holy shit. Holy, holy, holy shit.

Behraz Irani, woman of my dreams and filthy fantasies, has a crush on me?

CHAPTER 16:
YEARNING

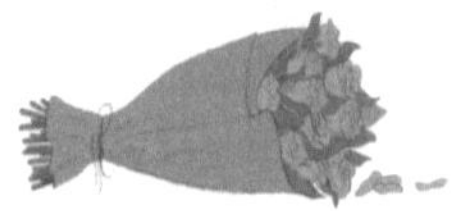

BEHRAZ

I'M SUDDENLY FEELING VERY POSSESSIVE OF Fletcher Donovan.

He's a shy, sweet, generous, incredibly hot hockey player who reads and has geeky quirks and is also a twenty-eight-year-old virgin. Like a unicorn in the wild.

If anyone gets to kiss him, or fuck him, or ride his perfectly rideable face, I want it to be me, and no one else. Good thing I offered up my body and then casually dropped I'm super into him. If he rejects me now, I'll have to change my name and go into witness protection.

There's too long a lull, and my fear grows, spreading like wildfire through my knotted yarn ball of a brain. I shift my grip on his hands, letting my thumb follow the speckled ridge of his knuckles. "Say something."

Fletcher's focus stays on a spot on the floor between our feet. "Just to be clear, *um*, I don't know what I'm doing." Same. His eyes flick upward, seeking contact. "But whatever it is, I know I want to be doing it with you."

Oh, thank fuck.

"Fletcher," I start, "Can I hug you now?"

He exhales through a soft smile. "Please."

I release our hands to wrap my arms around his waist and press my face into the planes of his warm chest, wanting to hear the steady beating of the gentle heart beneath.

Fletcher sweeps my loose hair away from where it gathers over my shoulders and rests his chin atop my head, his arms cradling my back.

We fit. I soak in the feeling: comfort, relief, content, all rolled into one. Nothing else matters; no world outside us exists.

An unexpected, high-pitched squeal from the hose has us jumping apart. We blush together. "Whoops, forgot to turn the water off."

I loop the pipe back on its stand and collect my bouquet from Fletch before locking up and heading back to his truck.

On the quiet drive back, his hand finds mine. Despite its large size, the contact is tender. The callus of his thumb draws a circle onto the skin of my left hand's ring finger, right above the knuckle. It's the second time he's done that, and I wonder why.

"What do you want for dinner?" Fletcher breaks the silence. "We can grab something on the way."

Who can eat at a time like this?

"I'm not that hungry, to be honest. I've got some leftovers I can turn into hot girl dinner."

"What's 'hot girl dinner'?"

I shrug. "There's cheese and crackers. And there are a few roasted Brussels sprouts I can shred."

A disapproving noise grumbles from his throat. "That's not dinner."

"I can make you something, if you want. I'm seriously not hungry."

I almost don't notice we've pulled into the parkade already.

"Absolutely not. I can make myself a smoothie and a sandwich."

"*Ooh*, Mr. Independent," I joke as we walk down the hallway to the apartment. "Do you feel like watching a movie with me while we eat?"

"*Hmm*. Depends."

"On?"

He steps through the doorway behind me. "The movie. I'm very picky, you know."

"I'm *so* sure. I've never seen you watch a movie."

"Excuse me, I was half-dead those first two weeks, and I am too much of a gentleman to say whose fault *that* was."

The back of my hand swats his arm. He doesn't flinch. I glower. "Y'know, I don't think I like this side of you." Liar. Pretty sure you like him more every day. "I've already said I was sorry about that. Multiple times."

"And I forgave you," he says with a polite half-bow, his eyes closed, "but that doesn't mean you can try to take advantage of my innocence under the guise of dinner and a movie." His hands clutch the crewneck collar of his tee, tugging it together as if to cover himself.

A horrendous, unladylike laugh bursts from me. "Have you always been this silly?"

"I beg your pardon! If this is your way of convincing me to watch a movie, you're going to have to try harder, Ms. Irani. I require effort. I require wooing."

He wants to play hard to get? I can court with the best of them.

"Fletcher," I coo. Three steps close the distance between us before my hand reaches for his bearded chin to brush over the soft hair with my thumb. "Do you wanna have dinner and watch a movie with me?"

He drops the charade, his body melting under my touch like ice cream on a hot day. "Yes, please."

"Good."

I flip through the options as Fletcher finishes making his turkey sandwich and settle on *Veer-Zaara* when he joins me on the couch.

"FYI, I do *not* approve of hot girl dinners."

Crispy bits of the Brussels sprouts crunch while I chew. "Good thing I'm a grown woman who doesn't require a man's approval."

"So sassy."

"And don't you forget it."

The title music of the 2004 classic plays. I back into the corner of the sectional, sitting with my legs crisscrossed and the dinner plate on my lap. Fletcher sits on the next cushion over, facing the TV.

"What's this movie about?"

"Yearning. And *shh*. There's no talking during movies."

We leave our plates on the coffee table once empty. My knees fold to my chest, and every few minutes, I shift a bit, feet getting closer and closer to Fletcher.

He inches not-so-subtly to me, too, and by the time Zaara leaves Veer at the train platform, my toes tuck under his warm thighs. Soon enough, I get the courage to position his arm around my knees. The weight of his bicep soothes me. His hand sweeps up and down my shin, easy and measured, further relaxing me into the plush sofa cushions. My eyelids get heavy during a conversation between Veer and his lawyer.

When they reopen, it's morning. The early rays fill the space through the floor-to-ceiling windows. I stretch my arms overhead and point my toes with a whine, escaping the chunky knit blanket covering me. Damn it, I fell asleep. And Fletcher didn't stay.

I check my phone for the time and see a reminder to go into work today. Shit. I told Theresa Giachetti I'd take care of scheduling before the office opens on Monday. A quick peek down the hallway tells me Fletcher's either not there or asleep. His bedroom door is closed. If I leave without showering, I can walk there, finish up, and come back in time to study.

Within thirty minutes, I'm at Giachetti & Associates, unlocking the glass front door.

DREAMBOAT

Where'd you go?

ME

The office

ME

I have to work for a couple hours

DREAMBOAT

Without me?

ME

Didn't wanna wake you, sleepyhead

ME

I can walk sometimes, you know

DREAMBOAT

What if someone kidnaps you?

I chuckle.

ME

> I can take care of myself

DREAMBOAT

> And what if I wanna take care of you?

Warmth pools in my chest. My face singes with a rush of blood to the surface of its skin.

DREAMBOAT

> Text me when you're done, I'll come pick you up

And I'm supposed to survive this?

CHAPTER 17:
SO, WANKING OFF 24/7 DOESN'T KILL YOU

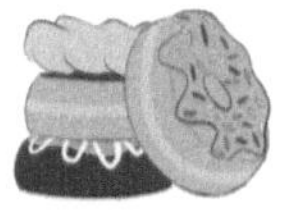

FLETCHER

I'M ON THE HIGHEST OF HIGHS.

She doesn't know how gone I am. She doesn't know that I imagined her face, her mouth, her tits, what she'd feel like, every time I fisted my cock in the past six years. Or that it's her name I moaned whenever I came for most of my adult life.

I do a few push-ups on the balcony to blow off steam while waiting for her to take a study break. The group chat blows up in the minute it takes me to do twenty. I scroll to catch up. Landon sent a family picture of him, Indi, and Akhila, all three smiling and framed by a reddish pink facade of a palace behind them.

LANDY

Look at this cute baby I helped make

BONER

God, I miss her sweet lil face

BONER

Cool palace bro

LANDY

How's it going over there

Wade sends a view of the golf course near his place in Fort Lauderdale.

BONER

Gabe is kicking my ass on the green today

LANDY

Just how you like it

BONER

Damn right

LANDY

Have you heard from Fletch?

LANDY

I haven't gotten an animal video in almost a month, and I'm worried

LANDY

Fletch?

LANDY

Buddy?

LANDY

You alive?

ME

Yeah, I'm alive

If they'd asked me three weeks ago, my answer would have been different.

BONER

So, wanking off 24/7 doesn't kill you

BONER

Good to know

ME

Shut tf up

LANDY

Yeah, he only does that 6 hours a day

I mean, he's not far off.

LANDY

Doing good?

ME

Yep

I wish I could tell them how good. But then I'd have to tell them about the concussion, and how Behraz is living with me. She'd kill me if Indi and Gabe found out because I blabbed to my nosy teammates. I can't out her and lose her trust like that.

Instead, I send them a reel of a group of otters slowly sliding across ice on their bellies.

ME

Us at dryland training next month

BONER

Tracks

LANDY

I'm the slowest one for sure

LANDY

My in-laws are hell-bent on fattening me up in the mother country

BONER

Shit, it's my turn to putt

BONER

My wife gets pissy if I take too long

LANDY

Title of your sex tape

ME

Title of your sex tape

LANDY

JINX 123456734056945863947530A9

BONER

middle finger emoji

The glass door of the balcony slides open, and I turn with a squint to reduce the glare of the sun.

"Fancy seeing you here," Bea sings.

"How's it going?"

"I submitted an appeal for the accommodations request. It takes three to six weeks for them to review it, so Dr. Gill has me trying some new methods." She slumps into the egg-shaped chair, drawing her knees into it. "The audiobook version of the manual seems to work better than visually reading the words."

"Good to hear."

"But for some reason, it's missing parts." Her mouth scrunches to one side. "Like it's an old edition or something."

"Weird."

"Right?"

Then it dawns on me. "What if I read it?"

"You'll read my exam prep for me?"

"Not *for* you, *to* you. Like a live audiobook."

"Wait, that's actually genius." Her hands clap together. "I could even record it and then listen to it at double the speed." The excitement drains from her face for a moment. "Are you sure you don't have anything better to do? It's all boring legalese—"

"I don't mind reading." I sit on my haunches in front of the chair, flanking her with my arms. "I can't think of a better way to spend my time."

Her feet slide down and rest on my thighs before she leans forward, hands cupping my jaw. I go lax into the light contact, no less than putty in her grasp.

"Okay, my little bookworm. Let's start now."

———

We don't get through enough material to choose a date that day, but I couldn't care less.

I spent the afternoon with her, watching her smile, making her laugh with my mispronunciations, cherishing the wrinkle in her brow, and the way her tongue pokes from the corner of her mouth when she concentrates hard.

It's like living in a dream. I never want it to end.

We've got the routine down. I drop her off at work, then hit the gym or go for a run, hop in the shower then circle back to pick her up. Or if it's Tuesday or Thursday, I drive her to therapy after making lunch together, then a few hours of studying.

"When I've got structure and routine, I thrive. And when I thrive, I'm happy," Bea said at the end of the first week.

That's what I thrive on. Being with her. Seeing her happiness.

It's a nice little life I could get used to. But the calendar on the fridge is a stark reminder that it isn't forever. An early date in August circled in red highlights her exam. I shrug the thought away. She's here now. Take what you can get.

Behraz dances into the kitchen, doing the Charleston with jazz hands. "Guess who aced their flashcards?"

"Good girl." The accidental praise has me hiding my face in my hands and my swelling cock behind the island counter.

Bea brings both hands to her mouth in a languid motion like that one shocked Barbie GIF. "My, my, my." She tugs her shirt away from her neck, fake-cooling off.

"I didn't...mean to say that."

"Too late," Bea teases. "It's stored in my memory forever. It's gonna come in handy one lonely night."

Sweat beads at my temples at the idea of Behraz touching herself at the thought of me praising her. The devilish smile across her face widens as she reaches for the date jar on the kitchen island. It rattles when she offers it to me. "Wanna choose? Or want me to choose?"

I close my eyes and grab a stick, narrowing my eyes to read the small handwriting. "What's tufting?"

"You're about to find out."

——

While I unlock the door, Bea hugs a tufted rainbow rug with smiley faces on the end clouds. "This is the cutest thing ever." She snuggles it once more. "I love it so much." The tufted yarn bends under the sweep of her hand. "It's gonna go next to my bed so my feet don't have to touch the cold flooring first thing in the morning."

Behraz could make me her bedside rug any time. I walk with her across the living room. "No hot girl dinner today?"

"That gelato *was* the hot girl dinner."

"I see."

"Fletcher," she starts, chewing on a corner of her beautiful lower lip. "I really, really, *really* wanna kiss you."

There it is. The beginning of the end.

"Oh."

This is what you wanted, Fletch. You want this.

"Are you scared?"

"Terrified."

"Of me?"

I reject the idea.

"You scared it might not be good?"

"A little." Yeah, what if I suck at kissing? I'd rather throw myself off a cliff than suck at kissing Behraz Irani.

"Okay, that's understandable. It's new and unknown. I mean, unless you don't want to kiss me—"

I half-sit on the arm of the sectional. "It's definitely not that."

She drops the rug to the floor and puts her hands around mine. "Then?"

"The bigger problem is that I...I've imagined this for a long time."

"First kisses are special, I get it." Bea plays with my fingers, stretching and curling them over hers.

"They are. But I meant with you."

"We only met last month." She steps between my bent knees.

All I can do is shrug. The admission is too hard.

"You've wanted me…longer?" Bea pries. "Months?" Her face tilts in question, so close I can taste the strawberry gelato on her breath. "Years?"

Our foreheads touch, and I still can't look at her. "If we kiss, I'm afraid I won't be able to stop," I whisper.

"That's okay by me," she whispers back. "Does that mean you want to kiss me? 'Cause I want you to kiss me."

"Yeah, it does. I mean, I do."

"Can I?" Behraz pulls my hands around her hips and rests her elbows atop my shoulders before tapping the middle of my forehead once. "Kiss you here?"

I nod, dipping downward. My eyes draw closed.

"Say yes."

"Yes."

Her lips move, feather-light against my skin, then purses to plant a kiss. A shaky sigh drops from my mouth. "How about here?" Two fingers coast over the top plane of my cheek.

"Yes."

Bea repeats the movement, and I shudder, bunching the hem of her shirt in my fists. It feels too good. She feels too good. "Here?" She draws a line to a spot at the corner of my jaw below my ear. My groin tightens. So does my grip on her waist.

"*Mmhmm.*"

I tremble through the kiss.

"Oh, my God, Fletcher," she says through a breathy giggle. "You're doing wonders for my ego." The column of my throat clenches through a swallow. "Hey, look at me."

I do, and I'm so glad. Her eyes go molten, nose sidling to mine, breath skating across the parted seam of my mouth. One of her hands bolsters my neck from going lax, while the opposite thumb sweeps over my lips. "Can I kiss you here?" The question is softer than a whisper. "It's easy, I promise."

"Please. Yes."

It begins pillowy, tender, a soft latch to my mouth that has my hands lifting to her face and hair. Then we're tugging closer and closer until we can't possibly be any closer. Surely we can't be any closer. We're breathing each other in and out.

I was right. I won't be able to stop.

A moan vibrates from my chest when her tongue sweeps over mine. Behraz echoes it with a delicious hum. "Fuck," I mutter. She tastes like warm paradise.

"Slip your tongue in my mouth," she directs.

I do. Each swipe is greedier, needier than the last, dragging the most maddening noises of pleasure from her. An aggravating ringtone from the phone in her pocket cuts us apart. "Sorry." She fishes the phone out. "Oh, shit. It's my parents."

"You...should take it."

Because my cock cannot take anymore. I sway back to my room after she closes her bedroom door, in a tizzy over this phenomenal kiss. My body goes limp against the mattress, but my dick is so hard it hurts. I silently scream into the pillow.

Behraz Irani kissed me. I kissed her. I may never sleep again.

CHAPTER 18:
WE CAN SAVE THE BLOWJOB
FOR ANOTHER TIME

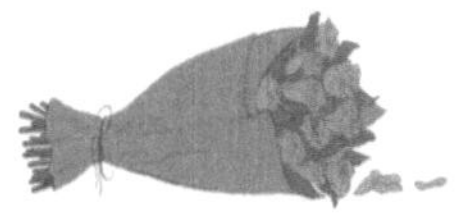

BEHRAZ

I'M NEVER KISSING ANYONE BUT FLETCHER DONOVAN ever again.

It wouldn't live up to it. Not even close.

I'm his first kiss. And he doesn't know it yet, but I'm sure as fuck gonna be his last. No way is anyone else ever gonna have sweet, perfect Fletcher Donovan after me. I shouldn't have picked up the phone. A ten-minute conversation turned into three hours, and then it was too late to recover what we started.

My thumbs hover over the keyboard in a message with Fletcher.

It's 7 a.m. He's gotta be up. If not, he'll see it soon enough.

ME

I can't stop thinking about last night

There's no response. Two minutes pass. I get impatient.

ME

Tell me I'm not imagining it

DREAMBOAT

Imagining what?

ME

I can't be the only one who can't
stop thinking about us kissing

DREAMBOAT

You're not

That's it. I'm going over there.

I dash to the door and open with an overeager pull, only to find a flushed Fletcher Donovan waiting for me on the couch.

My feet continue at their scurrying speed, before pouncing on the poor guy.

We crash together, mouths and teeth and tongues and tangled limbs. His hands roam from my face and through the mess of my hair, settling around my back to position me across his lap.

"I can't believe" —I gasp between brazen kisses— "you've never" —another gasp— "kissed anyone." He groans against my mouth. "You're so fucking good at it," I praise, nipping at his swollen bottom lip. "How is that possible?"

"Who fucking cares?" He laments, glassy-eyed. "Please don't stop."

I don't know if he means the praise or the kissing, so I keep going with both.

"You're sweet and gentle and kind and perfect," I continue, catching my runaway breaths between heavy kisses. "The color of your hair" —I swirl my fingers through the sides of it— "the splatter of your freckles" —the backs of my hands stroke down his pinked cheeks— "are what forlorn folk musicians write about. And these lips?" I draw two quick kisses from them. "How could they never have been kissed? I don't believe for a second that no one wanted to."

"Maybe they did, but *I* didn't want them to." Fletcher steals another kiss.

"Why not?"

He runs the tip of his nose back and forth across mine. "I wanted more than a kiss."

"A blowjob?"

"Fucking hell." His blush deepens, staining the shells of his ears with crimson. "No, I wanted someone to want me. For me. To know me and want me."

My palms uphold this sweet man's face. "I know you. And I want you. And I want to kiss you some more, too."

So, we do.

The alarm on my phone rings for me to get ready for work, but we keep kissing through giddy smiles and rolling giggles and tight cuddles.

"Okay, one more and then I *really* have to get ready for work." Fletcher tips my head up by the chin and makes the kiss count. "We can save the blowjob for another time, I guess."

————

How am I supposed to focus on studying now?

I can't even focus on getting out of the truck after Fletcher drives me home from the law firm. He kisses every knuckle, every finger, the inside of my wrists, all without breaking eye contact. "What're you thinking about?"

"So many things," I blurt. "But mostly about how you've got the prettiest pink mouth."

Fletcher freezes, his lips pressing against the throbbing pulse.

"And how pretty it'd look all over me."

Auburn freckles disappear behind the beet red of his blush. He curses under his breath.

"Can we go inside?" I ask, sounding whinier and more desperate than is usually acceptable. But the truth is, I *am* needy and desperate for this man. "I need you to keep kissing me, touching me, all over. Everywhere."

Fletcher lifts and tugs me across the cab, placing me in a straddle over his lap. "Can we take it slow?" His hands climb my thighs, dragging the hem of my dress upward.

"Of course."

"I wanna make you feel good."

"You do—"

"Teach me," he begs, burying his face into the crook of my neck. "God, I want you so badly. Tell me you want me, too."

I nod rapidly. "I want you."

"Tell me how." His plea fissures the weak walls of my heart.

I lift his head. "In all the ways I can have you. In all the ways that matter. Actually, in all the ways that don't, too. I want you in every way possible."

"Oh, thank God. Because you can have all of me."

I can?

"You hear me, Bea?" Fletcher catches my chin in the crook of his finger, forcing my gaze. "You have all of me."

CHAPTER 19:
DIP, DRIP, WET

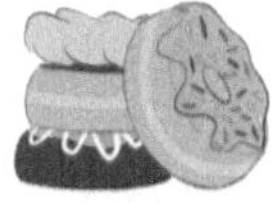

FLETCHER

MY DICK IS SO MAD AT ME.

Let's take it slow, you say. Fuck right off. Listen, my guy, we've been fine using our hands and imagination so far. A little longer won't kill us. *It might*, he protests.

We had to separate to get out of the truck, but instead of the couch, Bea sent me to my room with strict directions.

"Fletcher?" She knocks three times. "You changed?"

I smooth my beard and give my hair a last floof before answering the door. "Yep." I drag both hands down my sides. "Is this grungy enough for pottery throwing?"

She takes a step back and studies my faded Carhartt work pants and the plain tan tee with paint blotches on it from when we repainted my parents' house last summer. "Adorable."

We saunter to the spare room, which looks more like a paint and pottery studio with the wheel, clay, and some tools set up next to it. A clear plastic sheeting secured with blue painters' tape protects every surface: the floor, the walls, the bookshelves.

"Wow. You went all out."

"Anything to avoid clay stains. Exhibit A." She motions to the various spatters on her shirt and cuffed jeans. "Ready for your first lesson?"

I return a stiff salute. "At your command."

"Alright, have a seat on the stool. You're left-handed, right?"

"Yep."

"Lemme move the pedal" —Bea lifts the metal lever and wire over my head— "this is the pedal, by the way. It controls the speed of the wheel."

"Like a sewing machine."

"Kinda. That's your water." She points to a cloudy bowl. "Put a couple drops on the smallest circle in the middle there, then rub it around, enough to get it wet."

Fuck me. This was such a bad idea. I follow her direction, failing to subdue my horrendous blush.

"And here, here's your clay." She unwraps and hands over a formed ball. "Get a feel for it."

"It's heavier than I thought."

"Yep. Now here's the fun part. Slam it down into that circle as close to the center as possible." My arm lifts and turns to whack it onto the surface. "Easy, killer." Bea manually turns the wheel and adjusts the clay slightly to the left. "Your dominant hand will go here. But before you press the pedal, give that clay a smack."

I clap the top of it.

"Harder, Fletcher."

I'm so fucked.

"Like this." She demonstrates by raising her hand and slapping the clay so hard, it flattens.

"Jesus."

"That's how it's done." After putting a second stool down with a thud next to me, she sits. "Bring the water bowl to this side. Then start the pedal, and push all the way down, or else it's more work for you up here."

I do as I'm told. "I like when you're bossy."

"Stay on task, please. This clay is pricey, and it's all I've got left. Now, dip your fingers in the water and let it drip down your palms."

Yeah, I'm too immature and horny for this activity.

"Put your hands on it," she adds. "I'll show you how to make a cylinder first."

The clay is cool and firm and stays put, despite the high speed. Her hands join mine, keeping the round from going wonky under my heavy hand. "Not too hard. It only needs gentle encouragement. Use the heel of your hand to push upward."

It grows, taller and taller, but when Behraz lets go, I squeeze too hard, and the clay elongates into a flaccid penis flopping around everywhere. "Ahhh!"

"Let go of the pedal."

The spinning ceases, limp clay dick still staring back at me.

"Rookie mistake. Alright, that's okay. We'll start over." We repeat the same steps after Bea brings the clay back to a flattened ball shape. "Dip, drip, wet," she directs.

I clear my throat with a cough. "Has anyone ever told you that throwing pottery is strangely...suggestive?"

Her focus shifts from the clay to me, a wry smile perking the corner of her mouth. "Never heard that."

"You knew this? You're messing with me?"

"No, no. This is the terminology. Stop the pedal for a second. It's really uncomfortable to help you from the side." She ducks under one of my arms. "Sit back." Bea wiggles onto the stool between my legs, her back to my front, the ass of her jeans rubbing right up against...oh, no.

I contract every muscle, trying to give her some space, but there's none left on the wooden surface.

"Please don't move."

Her legs line up with mine, hands guiding me to the water bowl and back. She takes her fingers, along with two of mine, and dips them, pressing their wet tips into the peak of the cone we've formed on the wheel. The ends of her ponytail tickle my shoulder, and I nudge them away with my chin and short puffs of air.

"That gave me goosebumps." Bea extends her neck and pushes against me. "Do it again, but wet it first."

"Your neck?"

"Mmhmm."

The wheel whirs, pedal to the floor at the highest speed as my tongue licks a stretch of delicate skin beneath her jaw. I blow a breath over it. Behraz quivers against me. "Good?"

She nods. "Keep going." Her hands clamp over mine when my mouth grazes over the same spot. "Suck." I lick and suck, lick and suck, lick and suck until Bea writhes so much, my cock throbs from the friction. "Fuck," she rasps, releasing the clay, moving our muddy hands from her knees up denim-covered thighs. "Will you touch me, Fletcher?"

"Show me how."

One of her hands drags my damp, dirty fingers over her inseam. "Right here." The increasing pressure has her squirming and whimpering my name.

"God damn," I groan, then tongue over that sensitive spot on her neck again.

"Here, too," she murmurs, guiding my other hand to her chest. Her breast is soft and firm and heavy. I gasp. "Squeeze," she demands.

I mold it in my palm, tighter and tighter until it fills and spills over. Building pleasure sparks from my groin, winding and winding, nearly ready to explode. "Bea," I moan. She doles out the same treatment to my neck with her brilliant fucking tongue, and my head lolls to one side to allow for more.

My foot slides from the pedal, and we break free, her hands wrenching at my hair while I rub concentric circles against her clothed pussy, switching my free hand between her lush tits, leaving us both panting and sweaty and filthy.

"You feel so fucking good," I breathe into her ear.

She stills, her trim nails biting into my forearm when she lets go and finishes with a wince. I keep her flush to me, lips to her neck, every muscle juddering as my orgasm explodes. We collapse onto one another, and I sheathe her with my body. Her hand reaches for my cheek before she peers up at me.

"That was fucking fantastic." She beams, then pulls at the clay handprints on her chest and crotch. "You've made a mess of me."

"I guess we're even."

"How so?"

My eyes drop to my crotch.

Bea gapes, wide-eyed. "You...came?"

"In my pants."

"Holy shit. I barely touched you."

Oh, my God. I came on myself without her touching me. How's it gonna be when she actually touches me? My cock twitches in response. I'm fucking ruined.

"That is unbelievably hot," she continues. "And like I said, doing wonders for my ego."

———

At this rate, I'm miles ahead of the roster for dryland training. I'm so sexually frustrated, I double up workouts simply to rid myself of it. It's not particularly effective, but at least it gives me something to think about other than how stunning Behraz looks when she comes.

I finish lifting weights at the gym, but stay an extra hour, joining a group of guys on the basketball court who were short a player. The apartment is eerily quiet when I get back, and I think maybe I forgot about Bea's therapy appointment or something. My calendar says it's not until tomorrow.

I shrug to myself and opt for a freezing cold shower.

It's cut short when I hear a thud. Then there's a whine. I haphazardly dry myself and tug on a pair of sweats, racing across the apartment while imagining she fell in the shower again.

CHAPTER 20:
HELLO, POLICE? I'D LIKE TO FILE A REPORT

BEHRAZ

I WANT FLETCHER DONOVAN TO CATCH ME.

I want him to know how fucking crazy horny he makes me by merely existing. Too bad he's not around. And my favorite purple vibrator is nowhere to be found. I compromise on a set of nipple clamps and a slightly smaller blue silicone dildo. At least it vibrates.

All sweaty clothing of the day stripped and tossed to the floor, I sit my bare ass on the mattress and lean against the headboard. Licking my thumb and forefinger, I use them to work my nipples until they're hardened peaks between the metal bar piercing them. Getting the barbells helped recover the sensitivity lost when my boobs grew to their full size, but I'd already discovered clamps and didn't want to give them up. To accommodate for the piercings, this specific set connects with a delicate silver chain, somehow harsh and feminine at the same time. I spit to slick and tweak one side until my nipple shrinks enough to attach the clamp, then the other, sighing at the sting of pain they cause.

This dildo isn't as big as the rabbit, and doesn't stretch my mouth to the point of pain as I usually like. I do my best to wet it before turning on the vibration and moving it over each nipple, wishing it were Fletcher's rough hands instead. The buzzing coaxes goosebumps from my skin, and I widen the stance of my bent legs to slide the tip past the split of my cunt.

Arousal pools as I circle my clit, spreading the slick wetness over the sensitive, raised bundle. I bite back a moan and press the button again, upping the speed one level. The jolt is so strong, my head knocks into the headboard. A harsh squeeze to my breast induces a loud, achy wince. "Fletcher," I gasp.

"Fuck me," he replies.

My eyes fly open and immediately wrench shut, because there's no way the universe acted *that* fast over a wish. But when I reopen them, he's still there. Shirtless, panting, cock straining against the fabric of his sweats. His hands tear at his hair before dragging down his face. "What're you fucking doing to me?"

Momentary panic has blood pulsing in my ears. Get it together. You wanted this, Bea. The universe has given it to you; now make the best of it.

"To you? I'm doing it to *me*. I need this." I swipe the length of the toy through the wet layers of my pussy. "Wanna watch?"

"*God*, yes." The man whimpers and folds at the foot of the bed, holding himself upright on his hands, bowing toward me. It offers the most incredible view of his bare, heaving chest. His arms flex with restraint. "You think about me, Bea? When you touch yourself?"

"All the fucking time," I reply, thrusting the toy inside me at a languid pace. "I want it to be you."

"Fucking hell." His hips buck against the mattress, seeking contact. They match the speed of my thrusts, every roll straining the muscles in his torso.

"Oh, my God," I whine. "You're so hot." He grunts when I pick up the speed, plunging the toy through my pussy again and again. "You think of me, too?"

"Always," he heaves out.

My eyes stay on him, the synchronous rhythm taking me to the blissful edge of a massive cliff at a mind-numbing speed. His cock leaks, leaving a wet spot against the grey fabric of his pants. "That's right. Get that dick wet for me." I pump the silicone dildo deeper, increasing the vibration speed to its max.

"Fuck," he grumbles through his teeth. The sinews in Fletcher's neck go so taut I'm afraid they're gonna snap. "I'm gonna come, Bea."

"Want you to. Let go."

The swollen, red crown of his cock glistens over his waistband, spilling his release onto my pale pink sheets. He bellows a guttural groan. A jarring orgasm rolls through me at the sight. I release the clamps, the aftershocks so strong I nearly black out.

"That was," Fletcher mumbles, awestruck, "the fucking hottest thing I've ever seen."

I'm suddenly aware of my naked display and attempt to hide myself with my limbs. I'm not embarrassed about my body, but a part of me wonders if it's too much, too soon for him. We agreed to take it slow.

He answers by picking up the toy from the bed. "Can I use this on you?"

I would have never expected it. Bashful, blushing Fletcher Donovan asking to fuck me with a dildo. "Right now?"

"Right now." Neediness shakes his tone. "Teach me how you like to be touched. How to play with you, with this." He holds out the toy. I'm never gonna stop being wet at this point.

"Put it in your mouth," I urge.

Fletcher's eyes flutter shut with a moan as he sucks my cum from the silicone. "Now what?"

"Turn it on." It buzzes to life. "Feed it to me." He crawls closer on his knees and pushes it between my lips. I gag when it goes too deep. His hazel eyes gleam with wonder. "Where do you want to touch me, Fletcher?"

"Everywhere."

"Then do it."

He slides the toy down my chest, the vibrations against my sternum hardening my nipples once more. It circles my belly button before traveling lower. I seek something to grab, bracing myself. One hand lands on Fletcher's toned arm. The other clutches the top corner of my pillowcase. A bright red blankets his fair, speckled skin as he dips down, lifting a handful of breast to his warm lips. He moans, pursing around a tightened peak, doting on it with gentle lashes, flicking the metal bar with his tongue before leaving it with a harsh suck.

"Oh, my God," I groan. The rising pleasure sets fire to my skin.

Fletcher mouths the other side, mirroring his movements while drawing a line down my midsection. I wrap a hand around his wrist to guide him, urging the toy through the cleft of my pussy. My legs splay to allow entrance, but he doesn't push the fake cock in.

"Fucking look at you," he laments through a sigh. "You're fucking perfect." The praise has me impatient for more. He rolls the toy over my clit, once, twice, three times, so calculated and unhurried, I almost can't take it. "Where else can I touch you?"

"Inside me," I plead. "Put your fingers inside me."

He repositions himself, releasing the flesh of my breast to focus on my aching core. My hips lift when a slow drag of his callused finger teases the entrance. The walls throb, trying to pull the thick digit inside.

"Please, Fletcher." I'm not beyond begging for this man. "Please."

We gasp in tandem as one finger glides in without resistance.

"Fuck."

The rumbly curse and heightened speed of the vibrator on my clit make me clench around his inserted finger.

His eyes grow and flutter with every lazy drive in and out. "You feel incredible."

"Fletcher—don't stop. You're doing so well."

He hisses while pushing a second finger in, stretching my walls with the combined width. I let out a shameless moan. My eyes roll back when he moves them against the front wall of my cunt, unceasing vibrations over my clit rocketing me to the climax.

"I'm so fucking hard, Bea," he whines. "I'm gonna come again just from seeing you like this." But he doesn't stop. Instead, he presses the head of the silicone toy at the highest speed, right into the hood of my clit, quickening the movements of his fingers inside me.

"Fuck, fuck, fuck," I chant, arching from the bed as I spiral, tensing and shuddering without any semblance of control. A lilted cry of his name escapes me. Then, a sudden, surging stream.

When my vision returns, I'm wetter than usual. Shit.

Fletcher's jaw hangs open. "You...you..."

"Oh, fuck."

The pale pink of my sheets darkens to mauve. My hands rise to my sweaty, heated, embarrassed face. I squirted on this man the first time he fucked me with his fingers. He's probably shocked. And disgusted, he'll never want to be around me again.

"Unreal." Fletcher leaves a kiss on the inside of my bent knee. I jolt, still recovering from the orgasm. "Can...Can I eat you out?"

I simper.

Hello, police? I'd like to file a report against Fletcher Donovan. He's trying to kill me in broad daylight.

"Please?" His lush lips graze my inner thigh, nipping at the sensitive skin.

"I'm dying to know how you taste." My brain is empty. No words form in the post-orgasm haze. "Teach me, Bea. Teach me how to go down on you."

"Let me get cleaned up first." I go to straighten, but Fletcher stretches a hand across my stomach, the firm shove back to my reclining position low-key dominating. Hot.

"Later."

"But—"

He butterflies my legs and pins them with a gentle pressure, sliding down the bed until he lies on his front. "I want you to come all over my face like that." The filthy mouth on him. Surely this can't be the same Fletcher Donovan who couldn't speak to me for two weeks. "Tell me how."

I don't think I can. I'm too fucking turned on.

"Bea." His lips draw the whisper onto my flesh, prickling it with his beard and closing in on the space between my legs. "Tell me where."

My hand grabs a fistful of those incredible auburn strands atop his head, slotting his face exactly where I want him. "There."

He noses through the trim hairs above the split of my pussy lips.

"T-tongue," I stammer. He licks over my clit with a low moan. I gasp, grinding into him in response, but he keeps me spread open by circling his arms around my thighs. "Ssssuck." He does, and I might as well be dead because heaven is having this man's swollen lips on me. "Again."

"Been dreaming about this for years, Bea."

I twist and clench through a string of pitchy moans, fisting the sheets as he laps and laps and laps. My head whips forward to see his brows pinched together in a desperate expression. "Dreaming about how you'd taste, how you'd feel wetting my tongue." Another slow lash sweeps up my soaked cunt. "*God*, you're so soft. Smooth. Like silk." He groans and sucks my clit, deliciously rough. It catches me off guard. I hurtle through a blistering high, trembling in the aftermath as he cleans me with that wicked tongue. Weightless and dizzy, Fletcher sends my heart into a tailspin when I catch him licking my cum from his engorged lips, his beard streaked with my sticky release. He comes up for a searing kiss, coating my mouth with the sweet and slightly tart taste of myself.

It's too much, and the room darkens. Fletcher shushes my protest and envelopes me in a familiar warmth and the steady drumming of his heartbeat.

The next morning, I wake to a series of texts.

DREAMBOAT

Hope you got some well-deserved rest, gorgeous

DREAMBOAT

Had to go to the gym early today, but I'll be
back soon to go down on you again

DREAMBOAT

I need you to drown me this time

Fucking hell.

This is how I die, isn't it? I can see it now.

Behraz Irani, 27. Cause of death: spectacular cunnilingus.

CHAPTER 21:
WE'RE IN TROUBLE NOW

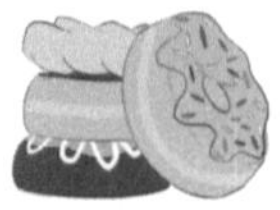

FLETCHER

BEHRAZ IRANI FUCKING OWNS ME.

Plus, I licked her cunt and got her to squirt in my mouth, so she's mine. She was a fantasy before. Now she's my reality. In a matter of weeks, she's become my everything. My roommate, my best friend.

Why didn't anyone tell me love and sex were gonna be like this? That this level of emotional intimacy was possible, and so quickly? Fuck, she makes me feel insane. Like a sex god...that hasn't had sex yet.

I don't even mind, honestly. Our daily routine got an upgrade. I still drive her to work, hit the gym, then shower, and come back to pick her up. Still take her to therapy. But the other days we return home, make lunch, then I read to her, or read on my own if she wants to study on her own. We make out, I eat her perfect pussy until we both come, and then we snuggle, clean up, and go to sleep. Lather, rinse, repeat until the weekend, when we choose a date idea and go on an adventure or play strip poker and eat food off each other.

If only that were enough. She deserves to know how I feel. She deserves all of me, even if it's not good enough. I slap myself during a pep talk in the washroom mirror, then point at my reflection. "Lock it in, Donovan. Channel Savage Garden and tell that woman you're truly, madly, deeply in love with her already."

And today's a good day to do so. To celebrate her finishing the prep manual material and finally getting her exam accommodations approved, I'm taking her to an ice rink.

"Ice skating?" she asked, reading the wooden stick plucked from the idea jar.

"Too lame?"

"Not at all, I haven't been in..." Behraz paused and searched the air, calculating.

"Then we're definitely going."

"I'll be out in a minute," she calls through the slightly ajar bedroom door. "You know, when I was younger, I was *obsessed* with ice skating. I took a few classes and thought I could be the next Michelle Kwan or Tara Lipinski. But my two left feet said, 'nope!'"

She struts out in one of her flower-patterned dresses. This green one is as wicked as the others. I swear she has one in every color and wears them just to torment me. She throws open the panels of a pastel yellow cardigan, running a finger down the few white buttons highlighting her full chest. Bea twists, showing off how the fluttery hem ends at the top of her thighs.

"What do you think?" She snaps a stretchy, nude fabric from her leg and wiggles her sock-covered toes. "Fleece-lined tights and thick wool socks so I don't get cold."

My last working brain cell explodes, draining its blood into my face and straight down to my dick.

She takes slow, slinking steps until she's right in front of me. "Fletcher." She tips my chin up with her petite palm, forcing eye contact. Her thumb strokes through my facial hair, waking goosebumps that run down my spine. "You're supposed to say you like it."

I relax into the tender touch. "I like it."

Behraz's eyes still for a moment, pupils blowing wide. Her tongue wets the seam of her rosy, stained lips. "Good boy."

In one feathery sweep down my neck, across the round of my shoulder, and down my arm, she takes control by clasping my hand, using it to help me to my feet and lifting it above her head so she can twirl.

"Can you see my ass?"

I check as we walk toward the door. "No."

"Damn. Well, does it at least look fat?" She leans in to whisper. "Say yes."

"Yes." I tease a grin and release our hands to slap the ample curve of her ass. She squeals in mock surprise. "And it's juicy, too."

"Me?" Her finger jabs one side of my butt. It jiggles. "What's all that movement back there?" She pokes it again as I'm pushing my foot into a sneaker at the door. I almost lose my balance. "The aftershocks are crazy." Her arms wind up like a softball pitcher and grip two handfuls of my ass. "This thing looks so delicious, I could just eat it. Om nom nom."

My cock pulses as we stroll down the hallway, asshole clenching at the thought of her mouth on it. "You can't stay shit like that to me, Bea."

"Or else?" She smirks, challenging my threat.

"Or else we're gonna have...trouble." If I get any harder, we'll have to go to the ER.

"Okay, okay. Let's get outta here. The site said public skate is only until six."

By the time we get there, all the ice scooters are rented out, so I skate backwards while holding both of Bea's hands. She pushes forward on the ice.

"You're doing great!" A couple of little kids zoom past us without any aid, shaking their heads. Behraz throws me a doubtful look. "Don't pay any attention to them."

"I'm not."

"You have nothing to be ashamed of—"

"I know..." She stifles a smile, driving her skates harder, forcing me back. "I actually don't need help."

"You don't?" I pick up speed to keep up with her. "What about your two left feet?"

We turn around the curve.

"I'm no Michelle Kwan, but I'm not terrible."

I release one hand to skate alongside her as she speeds through center ice.

"But then you held my hands and were being so cute, so I went along with it."

Wow. I'm an idiot.

"I'm Canadian, after all. It's pretty much a requirement to know how to ice skate." She leans forward and balances on one foot, raising a leg behind her. "Indi, Gabe, and I go down to the canal every winter. Don't worry, Fletcher. I like it when you hold my hands."

Despite the frigid air around us, my skin flames.

"And I like how flustered you get even more." She tugs my arm to whisper in my ear. "The way you blush is so hot."

"We're in trouble now," I mutter. "We're gonna have to go home."

"*Oooh*," the instigator says through a giggle. "I like a little trouble."

"It's about to turn into more than that."

We're in big, massive, rock-solid trouble.

———

We stumble through the entryway, lips locked and tongues tangled as we kick off our shoes.

Bea escapes and beats me to the bedroom. I pant in the arch of the open door, watching her strip away her socks and leggings in the dressing mirror on one side of my bed. She reaches below the fabric and pulls down, retrieving a flimsy lace string that slips to the floor.

I gulp.

"Fuck." My hand scrubs my face. "That dress is killing me."

"I should get rid of it, then." She undoes one button. "I don't want you to die." Then another. And another, and another, and another, and another, until a sheer, strapless bra appears, cutting through a creamy stretch of her midsection as she bunches the flowery fabric to her hips. Her arms pretzel behind her, unhooking it to remove from the front, revealing those mauve nipples pierced with shiny metal. She throws it to the side and crawls onto the bed. Her tits sway with every stalking movement toward me.

"God." I give my solid cock a squeeze over my sweats.

"That's so hot," Bea coos, kneeling atop the edge of the mattress. "Come here," she beckons with a curled finger. "Take off your shirt."

Hell, I could come right now. But I obey, shrugging off the flannel button-up and the white tee below in one swoop over my head as my feet guide me to her.

"You can have whatever you want from me, Fletcher." Her eyes dart back and forth between mine. "Just say the words. Tell me what you want."

"I—" Don't have a functioning brain right now.

She toys with a piercing. "You wanna touch them?"

I nod rapidly.

"Words, Fletcher."

"Yes," my voice rasps, unrecognizably low.

She circles both wrists and places my palms over her breasts. My fingers stretch and contract around the soft flesh, warm and lush in my grasp. I suck in a shaky breath. Her nails scrape along the elastic securing my pants to my hips. I hiss when they cross the line of hair above my groin.

"You want me to suck your cock?"

The question and mention have it straining in my boxer briefs.

"God, yes."

"Then take it out."

I lower the band, and it springs forward, the swollen head overeagerly leaking with pre-cum.

"Holy shit," she gushes, switching her focus from its length up to my face. "You're already that desperate for me?"

I nod again, muting a groan while thumbing over her tightened nipples.

"You make me so fucking wet, Fletcher."

My cock bobs midair at the idea.

"Wanna see?"

All I can do is verbally agree. I'll give this goddess whatever she fucking wants.

Bea scoots back, getting on all fours, then flips up the skirt of that dress to give me the most illicit view of her dripping pussy in the mirror behind her.

"Fuck," I lament, stroking myself.

"Fuck," she echoes. "Grab my hair, Fletcher."

I gather it gently, but it's so thick, so voluminous, I struggle to fist it all. Impatient, she wraps it around my wrist. "Tighter," she demands. "You're...bigger than I imagined. But I don't care." She confirms with a hungry look. "I want you to go rough. Use me—please, Fletcher."

"Bea?" She winces when her coiled hair goes taut in my grip. "I know you know what you're doing, but..." I pump down my length once, spreading my arousal while nearing her mouth. "I need you to listen."

Lust and need swirl in her blown gaze. "Tell me how to suck you off."

I offer my glistening cock to her. "Lick it."

The long, languid swipe she doles out has me quaking out a moan.

"Take it in your mouth."

Her lips wrap the engorged head with a weak suck.

"Harder."

The pressure intensifies. My head lolls back with a pleasured hiss as the thick vein lining the underside of my cock throbs on top of her tongue.

"Deeper."

Her mouth is hot and slick and unbearably snug. "Fuck," I groan when she retreats, only to see my cock disappear further past her lips. "Can you take more?"

She nods with an *mmhmm*, the vibrations onto my cock making the room spin temporarily.

"Good," I affirm. "You look incredible with me filling your mouth."

Bea moans, and I can barely hold on. "Keep going."

Every intake pairs with a blissful hum, barreling me towards a release. But I don't want it to end yet. I shiver, attempting restraint with a pause, posting my free hand onto her shoulder. She draws me in until I reach the back of her throat, then chokes. My cock isn't even slotted in the whole way, but the sheer sound, *fuck*.

Watching her cunt drip down her thigh in the mirror was a mistake. Something inside me snaps, like a rabid, caged animal finally breaking free from its enclosure. I hold her in place, recreating the feeling with a harsh thrust. She gags, covering my cock in a fresh coat of her spit. "Oh, fuck, *yes*." My other hand joins its twin, winding into the silken strands. "I'm gonna fuck your face now, okay?"

She nods silently, tears pooling, strings of spit starting to dribble from her lips. A fucking fantasy comes to life. I whimper. My hips drive forward, the cadence hasty, greedy for the sloshy clucks from pushing my cock deep into Bea's throat. Moan after moan pours out of my locked-open mouth, shameless and loud, like the sweat down my torso.

Her sucking strangles my length with a heavenly pressure, balls recoiling as the mounting pleasure at the root of my spine readies to burst. All it takes is for Bea to whine, and I freeze into a forward curl, trembling while releasing white hot streaks of cum into her perfect mouth. Tears stream down those pretty pink cheeks, her lips swollen from my unyielding abuse.

"Wait." I grab her throat as I pull out lazily, a thick rope of my cum still connecting us. "Let me see."

She widens her mouth, presenting my cum on her tongue.

"Now swallow." It vanishes as I urge it down the rigid column of her neck with my palm. My cock twitches at the sight.

Behraz returns a dazed chuckle. "That's the most erotic thing that's ever happened to me."

"You're unbelievable," I coo, plucking a greedy, tongue-filled kiss, then wrench her dress higher up her back. The relief post-orgasm has me all fucked up. "Now turn around. I'm gonna clean you up."

———

Hearing Behraz cry out my name while eating her cunt from behind almost ends me.

Behraz's naked chest bathes in an afterglow, both from her orgasm and the setting sun outside the window.

"Is there anything else you want to try with me?" Her hand courses down my bare torso, combing through the long hairs between my pecs.

I want to try—do everything with her. It's what I want to say. It's what I should say. But we've fed the beast too much, and I suggest something else entirely, like a greedy, heinous monster. "I wanna fuck your tits."

Behraz doesn't miss a beat. "You want me on my back or on top?"

The urge for control holds strong. "On your back."

"Take off your pants." She rolls and shifts downward while I do. "Put your knees here." Bea pats the mattress on either side of her hips. I get into position, cock in hand stiffening at an astonishing rate. Behraz Irani's tits are a fucking gift. She spits on the head. "I've never done it before, but…" The thought of being the only person to have her like this has my balls aching, cock pulsing. More saliva joins my length. "…I think we might need some lube."

I lean over to the nightstand and pull a tube from the top drawer. She uncaps it to squeeze a fat line of it onto her finger, then tosses it aside to slather the glaze generously between her breasts.

"Put your cock here," she directs, bringing the rounds together.

My eyes close by instinct as I push my cock into the small space. She holds them tight as I grind my hips through while mumbling a string of curses. With each thrust, she lashes the tip of my cock with her tongue, turning me into a grunting, groaning mess of a man in a matter of seconds. I inch closer and closer to the edge, the muscles of my arms shaking. The last few drives get sloppy, and when Bea's eyes roll, I let go with a scream.

My cum stripes her chest in white.

"Oh, my God," she exclaims, peering down at my release and sweeping a finger through its stickiness. "That was so quick."

I recline on my haunches, still straddling her, my lifeless cock lying against her belly. "See what you fucking do to me?" My hands spread the slick all over her tits, wanting to mark her as mine. "You own me."

She simpers when I gloss over her dark pink nipples and pinch their metal piercings before mouthing one. I leave it with an intense suck, soothing away the pain by stroking my tongue over the taut nub, before moving onto the other side.

"I'm gonna" —her body bows toward my mouth— "I'm gonna come, Fletcher." Both of her strong hands tear at the sweaty, tousled hair topping my head, filling my cock with blood once more. She stiffens beneath me, toes curling, then lets out an extended scream.

I lick her skin clean, savoring the taste of my own cum as my cock reaches the bare, drenched split between her legs. "Can I kiss you now?"

She's still recovering from the high. "You want to...kiss? After...?"

I cradle her sweet face, an afterglow in and of itself. "Don't you want to taste us, Bea?"

"I do."

We share a heated kiss before she loses consciousness. There's an insane smile slapped on my face. I, Fletcher Donovan, a twenty-something virgin, have made Behraz Irani, sex goddess extraordinaire, pass out from pleasure.

When I slink off the bed and into the washroom, I force out a silent, excited scream while knocking my knees together in a dance of victory. After wiping us both down with a warm washcloth, I dress her in my jersey from her room and tuck her into my bed. I gulp down three glasses of water, grab a bottle of alkaline water, and leave it at her bedside with a protein-packed granola bar. If she wakes before sunrise, she's gonna need it.

I pick up *Lore of the Tides* and recline next to her sleeping form, and we're both exactly where we belong.

CHAPTER 22:
SPIRAL INTO THE CHAOS

BEHRAZ

WHATEVER PART OF MY BRAIN IS RESPONSIBLE FOR emotional regulation is on the fritz.

Stress from the fast-approaching bar exam has me so unstable; all it took was a call from my brother asking how studying was going for me to have a full-on mental breakdown on the couch.

I'm talking uncontrollable sobbing, endless snot, dozens of used tissues, and a foul odor emanating from my mouth because I've been too occupied with crying my eyes out to get out of bed and brush my teeth.

"Bea?" Fletcher calls from behind my closed door. Sweet, patient man. I squeeze out hot tears thinking about how lucky I am to have someone who gives a shit, even though I don't deserve to. "Can I come in?"

"No, it's a mess." I don't want him to see me like this again.

"I don't mind."

I do need him. "Okay," I wail.

With one look at the sad state of me and my room, his expression softens from worry to compassion. "Oh, sweetheart."

He toes over old pizza boxes and piles of books while my arms lift for a hug, like a child, and Fletcher scoops me up as if I weigh nothing, sweeping away my dirty laundry to return us to bed in the cocoon of his wide chest. I curl into it, burrowing my face in the cozy crook of his neck.

"What happened?" One large hand coasts down my back with a shush, slowing the rapid pace of my breathy sniveling. "You're scaring me."

"What—if—I—fail—again?" I push out a ragged exhale.

Fletcher dots kisses across my forehead, the warmth of his lips drying its clammy surface.

"All those years I was told I was quirky. 'Silly, clumsy, forgetful, chaotic, screw-up Behraz,' but it was my brain all along. What if I spiral into the chaos again? Then what? I try again, fail again? And keep the circle of disaster going?"

"It's a valid fear, but that's not going to happen," he assures, pushing back the damp hairs stuck to my face with tears.

"It's a goddamn mess. I'm a mess."

"You're not a mess."

I peek up at him, tears sitting on my lashes and snot streaming onto my lips, and move my head around my disgustingly messy room.

He huffs out a laugh. "Okay, you're a little bit of a mess. But you're *my* mess, and I don't mind it one bit." Fletcher thumbs a fresh tear away. "It's gonna be better this time. You have accommodations and more professional and academic support than before."

I agree with a slow series of nods.

"And I'm here, too."

"What if you get tired? Gabe and Indi have no clue, and they have enough responsibilities in their lives. They have jobs and families and partners, and how much can they do anyway? I'm too much to take care of. My own parents don't want to deal with—"

"Behraz." He silences me with a finger to my lips. "You're not too much." I accept the kisses he plants on my eyelids. "Getting to take care of you is my favorite thing."

I shed a few more tears at his devotion, letting him baby me until I'm calm. My tears soak the collar of his tee.

"God, I've been rambling for, like, hours now. You must be so over it."

"Why would I be?"

"Because I'm annoying, I just yap, yap, yap, on and on and on..."

"Someone said that to you?"

I shake out a weak shrug.

"Talk all you want, gorgeous." Fletcher dips down, pressing his lips against the curve of my ear. "Your voice makes my dick wet."

A cackle escapes me. I'll never get over this shy man's dirty talk. "Fletcher." My hands cup his face as I tease a kiss from his velvety lips.

This man has seen all my nasty, ugly, messy parts and still acts like he's the lucky one for being stuck with me. "I'm not convinced I'm any good for you, but I want you to know" —I tap our foreheads together— "I'm really, really stupidly in love with you."

Fletcher beams against my mouth, gushing out a minty breath. "I love you," he says softly, sharing a secret that's meant only for me. "I wasn't living before you. Simply surviving. You nearly killing me with your bike..." He pecks the tip of my nose and the apple of each cheek. "You brought me to life, Bea. When I say I've been obsessed with you for years..." He shakes his head. "I know it's pathetic, but I don't care. I'm pathetic when it comes to you. Do you remember going to a club called Persepolis with your friends?"

My eyes widen with recognition, parting my mouth with a gasp.

"I saw you. It was the drunkest I've ever been, and I didn't have the guts to come up to you, despite my friends' best efforts." His fingers loop through mine, shifting his focus between us. "You were—*you are*—literal sunshine in the dark cloud of my sad little existence. The way you laugh?"

"Like a witch?"

He rejects the suggestion. "Like you're free. Free to be happy, to live life on your own terms. And your smile?" It widens with the praise. He exhales with a low whine. "You're the brightest star in my sky."

"Why are you so sweet to me?"

"Because you don't deserve anything less. I've watched you—admired you from afar for so long. Saw how you're a loyal, supportive, protective friend. Your determination, like nothing is too big a challenge or too serious not to laugh through. You're all the things I have no idea how to be. You make people feel welcome, like they belong with you. And you fit in, in any place, get along with anyone you meet. You could've had anyone, and you chose me?" He huffs out a laugh. "Most days, I can't wrap my head around it. I can hardly believe that you're...mine."

It's the first time he's said it. No one else has said it before. The next few tears that escape from the corners of my eyes warm my soul. "Say it again."

"You're mine." He fixes his gaze on mine, brimming with unadulterated adoration.

"I love being yours."

"Can I be yours?" he asks. "It's all I want, Bea."

I nod against him, keeping our faces slotted together. "It's all I want, too. You're all mine."

His hold tightens, secure and persistent.

"Can I tell my friends?"

"Tell whoever you want. Hell, let everyone know."

"What should I say?"

"That I belong to you."

"And no one else?"

Fletcher seals the promise with a breathtaking kiss. "And no one else."

———

The opportunity to do so comes quickly after Gabe and Indi return to Ottawa. I got so anxious about being late, since I'm always running late, that I got there fifteen minutes early, and forgot they don't give tables at Wilf and Ada's until the entire party is there. I manage to convince one of the usual servers to give it to me anyway.

INDI BHINDI

Running late for brunch!

INDI BHINDI

It's Akhila's fault. She always poops whenever I have to be somewhere on time.

GABE BABE

First of all, how dare you??

GABE BABE

Second of all, I know you did not blame my angel baby.

GABE BABE

Lastly, I, too, am late. My husband was horny.

ME

No worries, I'm at our table already

ME

Laura hooked us up

They react with surprised emojis and a million exclamation marks.

INDI BHINDI

What's going on?? Are you okay??

GABE BABE

Never thought I'd live to see the day

ME

Hilarious!!!!!!!! (sarcastically)

INDI BHINDI

I'll be there in 2 mins

INDI BHINDI

COMING TO RESCUE YOUUUU

GABE BABE

From what??

INDI BHINDI

Whoever is holding her hostage

One of our usual servers approaches to refill my water, and I hold a hand over the rim to stop her. "I'm good, thank you." When Laura turns toward the kitchen, I refocus on my phone. I can't believe *I'm* the calm one on the group chat right now.

"Okay, I'm here." Indi loops her crossbody over the chair and takes a seat. "Tell me everything."

"What happened to 'hello, how are you?'"

"Hello, how are you?" Gabe hugs me from behind and sits next to me. "Now, spill."

"Hold that thought. I'm so hungry I could eat this whole restaurant." Indi calls over the familiar waitress. "Hey, Laura. Could I have a mimosa, please?"

"That's not food," I comment. It's also an $11 drink I can't afford at the moment.

"Make it two," Gabe adds. "And an order of avocado eggs."

"Sure thing, what about you?" Laura asks Indi.

"I'll take a benny today. Florentine."

"With homies or greens?"

"Both."

"I'm not ready!" I blurt, unprovoked, taking the three by surprise. Smooth. So chill of you, Bea.

Laura gives us a polite smile. "I'll...bring out your drinks and have them start on the order. Lemme come back after a few minutes to circle back."

As our server walks away, Indi narrows her eyes at me. "I was joking before, but now I'm actually worried about you."

Laura swings by again to drop off glass flutes filled with their mimosas. Indi rushes it to her mouth, nearly spilling it onto her lap. She takes a swig and lets out a contented sigh.

I slide a concerned look to Indi. "I thought you can't drink while nursing."

"You can't. I'm gonna pump and dump. I have an *insane* amount of stored breastmilk, a whole deep freezer full. Plus, Akhila eats real food now. She's gonna be fine." She and Gabe clink glasses and take simultaneous sips.

For the first time in my life, I'm speechless. I don't know where to start. So much has happened in six weeks.

"Behraz?" Indi's voice cuts through my wandering train of thought.

I feel like I'm torn apart, being ripped in half like a thin sheet of paper. My mouth quivers into a frown, clinging to a thread of control that's ready to break.

"Oh, girl." She comes around to this side of the table to wrap me in a hug while we share the seat.

I tell them everything.

About the ADHD diagnosis and getting kicked out of my sublease. How I moved my stuff in Parvez's bakery back office using Landon's Range Rover.

"I wanted so badly to tell you, but..."

"The less I know about the Rover, the less Landon knows about it."

"Fuck," Gabe breathes out. "You know you're welcome to stay at our place anytime."

"Same goes for us." Indi squeezes my shoulder and kisses my temple.

"I didn't want to be a burden."

Indi's eyes go watery, refreshing the tears streaming down my cheeks. "You're no one's burden, Bea."

"We're not blood," Gabe confirms. "But you're still family."

"Where the hell have you been staying?" Indi pauses, then shakes her head. "Never mind, I don't wanna know."

I promise you, you definitely want to know.

"You're coming home with me right after this. I have the minivan. We can grab your things from your brother's store."

"That would be a good plan," I say through a sniffle. "If my stuff was there."

Gabe's brows rise. So do Indi's.

"There's more..."

Indi sucks in a breath and swivels back to her chair across from me.

"I was coming back from my ADHD therapist one day, and I was riding my bike too fast and not paying attention..."

"Oh, God, are you okay?" Indi searches my body.

"I'm fine, I'm good." I hold up both hands to keep her calm. "I'm great, actually."

"You're great?"

"You'll never guess who I nearly took out."

Gabe's palm smacks the width of her forehead. "We're brunching with a bike assaulter."

Even the thought of his name stretches my face into a smile. "Fletcher Donovan."

"That's a shit-eating grin if I ever saw one" —Indi hums out a series of disapproving noises— "What have you done?"

———

"How big?" Gabe positions her hands in the air in front of her, widening the space between them to show length. "Tell me when to stop."

I don't. At least not until she passes the diameter of her lunch plate.

"Jesus. He's bigger than Wade."

"For sure," Indi confirms.

Gabe and I whip our heads to her.

Gabe glowers at her. "How would you know?"

Indi shrugs through a bite of salad, then swallows. "The first time I met Landon and Wade was in the locker room. They were both naked as the day they were born, bakery and deli on full display."

"*Ohhh*, yeah," Gabe intones with a long, slow nod. "Wade mentioned that sometime ago. I kept forgetting to bring it up."

"Don't tell Landon, but Wade is definitely bigger." Indi's eyebrows jump once as she takes a long sip of her drink. They both move their focus to me. "That means Fletcher is..."

"...the biggest." Gabe finishes the statement. "It's always the shy ones, isn't it?"

"I mean, don't get me wrong. I'm good with Landon's larger-than-average size. I don't need monster dick," my friend says a little too loudly, earning some curious looks from a nearby table.

"Thoughts and prayers." Gabe leaves a few comforting pats on my back.

Indi takes the last glug of her second mimosa. "R.I.P. your vagina."

"We...haven't slept together yet." The admission has me feeling bashful. Me. Behraz Irani. My face flames. "We're taking it slow."

"I'm glad." Indi clasps my hand over the tabletop.

"I'm in love with him," I add.

"We know," Gabe adds through a laugh. "You two finally got it together. We've been rooting for you guys for years."

"Really? I had no idea."

"Oh, yeah. Wade has been trying to get Fletcher to talk to you forever. You two are made for each other."

"We are, aren't we?" I beam. "I'm glad you approve. He's literally the best thing to ever happen to me."

"And he's lucky to have you, but that doesn't change what I said," Gabe breathes through her nose through a drink of water. "I'm still praying for you. Whenever you decide to do the dirty, Fletcher Donovan's gonna have you limping around town for a week afterward."

Indi chokes. I almost do a spit take, and all three of us break out into a collective cackle.

I'm banking on it.

CHAPTER 23:
YOU HAVE A KINK

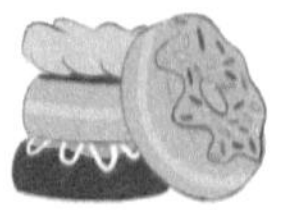

FLETCHER

"I WANNA FUCKING DIE," LANDON SAYS THROUGH quick, leaden breaths, after completing a series of agility ladders. "This new drills coach can fuck right off."

"Next time, lay off the ladoos, Landy." Wade straightens, keeping his hands on his hips. He's a goddamn poet.

Jaeger grunts, seemingly unshaken by the exercise. Our team's captain is 6'6, 230 pounds, and barely breaking a sweat.

"I would, but they sent us home with a hundred-pound box of them." Landon shakes his head. "Poor Esha."

"Who's Esha again?" I ask.

"Indi's youngest sister," Landon explains. "She's the whole reason we all went to India."

"Oh, right. She got married or engaged or something?"

He denies it. "Nope. The groom-to-be and his family were being pricks about an enormous dowry. Indi's parents essentially called it a stupid, outdated tradition they didn't believe in, but the guy's side apparently expected thousands of dollars and lavish gifts. It turned into, like, a *huge* thing, and her parents told them their daughter wasn't for sale."

"That's horrifying. I mean, for her family."

Landon takes several gulps of Gatorade. "She ended up breaking it off, and we went on a family trip through Rajasthan instead." My friend has become quite the gossip queen in his old age. "They tried to get her to come back to Canada with us, but she went on a Paris honeymoon. Said she paid good money for it and wasn't gonna let it go to waste over a piece of crap like her ex."

One of the d-men, Olsen, jogs by with a dopey grin, pushing out a series of equally dopey chuckles. It only takes a second to realize we've been crop-dusted. We struggle to protest, choking on the residual fumes.

"Aw, come on, man!"

"That's fucking rank!"

We get yelled at for lollygagging and get thrown into the burpee corner of the field, and when the fifty-count punishment is completed, we lie on our backs against the grassy slope.

Not wanting to get sunburnt to hell, I crawl into the nearest shade, cast onto the lawn from the training facility. Jaeg takes off his shirt and basks in the sun, tucking his arms behind his head. Landon curls into a fetal position, the color draining from his face, threatening to vomit.

"Fuck you, you chatterbox," Wade curses Landon. "Donny," he heaves. "What's going on with you?"

Might as well spill it. "Bea's my girlfriend."

Landon huffs. "Eh? I think I'm losing it because I thought I heard you say Bea was your girlfriend."

"I heard the same thing," Wade adds. "You delirious, man, or what?"

"Nope, this summer, well...long story short," I stumble through an explanation, "we were temporary roommates, but shit happened and now we're permanent roommates."

The goalie lets out a weak *woo*. "Fucking *finally*."

"I'm so happy for you." Landon crawls slowly closer to me, his face ashen with nausea. "So excited I could throw up. Know that in my head, I'm whooping and galloping around like a show stallion."

"Has your dick fallen off yet?" Leave it to Wade to ask the important questions.

"Almost," I pant, the heat clearly cooking all my brain cells. My mouth runs without any trace of impulse control. "*God*, she's amazing. She makes *me* feel amazing. I'm so fucking in love with her."

Wade feigns surprise with a melodramatic gasp. "No shit? I never knew. It's like all you had to do was give it a chance or something."

"Blow me," I retort.

"Hell no. I'm not doing your girlfriend's dirty work for you."

My girlfriend. *My* girlfriend. Mine. I'll never get over calling her mine.

"What he means is" —Landon rolls to clap a sweaty palm to my shoulder— "we're happy for you."

"Thanks, man."

"And welcome to the club."

A whistle blows to call us back to the coaches. In the past few years, dryland training didn't start until September, but two weeks weren't quite enough to prevent injuries during exhibition games and prepare us for the regular season. Since we didn't make it past the first round of playoffs, team management has us training in late July to give us more time to shape up post-vacation.

Damn. Only two weeks before Bea moves out. A whistle cuts my wallow short.

"We'll meet at the CTC tomorrow. Stay hydrated and get ready for box jumps."

We break from the huddle and move towards the parking lot. Landon shuffles back to his Range Rover, visibly stiff and sore. "I hate everything."

Wade, the flexible bastard, stretches a leg on the hood of the Rover he got last year. I swear, goalies are built different. "Get it together, old man. This was only the first day."

Jaeger holds up a hand to wave goodbye before wordlessly getting into his Jeep.

"Jaeg seemed quiet, even for him," I comment.

"You're right. Wonder what's up with him." Landon watches the captain drive off. "I'll ask Indi if Skylar's mentioned anything."

I check missed messages when getting back into the cab of my F-450.

> **GORGEOUS**
>
> All done for the day?

> **ME**
>
> Yep

> **GORGEOUS**
>
> How was training?

I send back a video of a family of otters chasing a butterfly.

GORGEOUS

Not sure I understand, but how cute!!

ME

It's me and the guys trying to win the Stanley Cup

GORGEOUS

This is your year!!!!

ME

Did you tell your friends?

GORGEOUS

Oh yeah

ME

How'd it go?

GORGEOUS

I had a meltdown and told them everything

GORGEOUS

So, as expected

ME

???

She replies with a GIF of someone sobbing next to Selena Gomez, then another one of Meryl Streep cheering with a single clap and pointing ahead, subtitled in yellow font with the word, "*Yes!*"

ME

Haha

GORGEOUS

I had no idea they were such big fans of Fletcher Donovan, but they're not wrong for it

ME
Stop, I'm blushing

GORGEOUS

When are you NOT blushing??

That's fair.

ME
I can't help it with you

GORGEOUS

I know, and it makes me horny as hell

My cock fires up.

GORGEOUS

When are you heading home??

ME
Right now

GORGEOUS

Good, cause I miss you

ME
running emojis

I rush down the hallway, already bricked the fuck up from imagining how sweet my girlfriend's cunt is gonna taste on the island counter, but my pace slows when I hear a deep bass vibrating the walls leading up to the apartment. Dance music blasts through the open door, drowning my footsteps out. So focused on her task, Bea doesn't notice me coming in.

Blood pumps straight to my cock at the sight of her wielding a chef's knife. She studies the weight of the wooden handle, flipping it in her palm before a deft twirl through her fingers returns it to a solid hold. Oh. "Volume, ten percent." The music softens at her command. "Hey, Dreamboat."

Messy ideas popping up within my head scatter at the casual, off-the-cuff greeting.

"I'm so glad you're home."

"Me too," I say, stupefied. Deranged thoughts return to fill my brain as her swift, steady movements slice through an eggplant.

"So, you have a kink." Behraz lifts her narrowed gaze, without breaking the stride of her blade.

My eyes blink, blink, blink in shock. She *did* notice. Way to go, Mr. Inconspicuous.

Her lips smirk. "Is it me being in the kitchen, or something else?"

"I—*buh*." Words fumble from me.

"This is probably the third time I've seen you hard when I chop something."

A blush flares. Let's be honest, I'm always hard around her, but when she's holding a knife? I might as well finish in my pants. Wouldn't be the first time and won't be the last.

"I-I like knives." The explanation comes out monotone and dopey. Clearly, blood is not recirculating back to my brain.

She perks an eyebrow, pausing before the next cut. "I see." The end of the eggplant slices away. "Lucky for you," she discards it into a pile of scraps, "so do I."

I whimper.

Bea's smirk turns villainous. She could do literally anything she wanted to me, knife or otherwise. "It's always the shy ones" —the knife points in my direction, accusing— "y'all are big-dicked, chock-full of secret kinks and vivid imaginations."

My cock weeps, knees buckling so quickly I have to use the counter for support.

"If I didn't have ten more minutes left on this chicken parm in the oven..." Her sentence trails off with a sharp *whew* through those pink pursed lips.

Restraint thrown aside, I pounce over the granite-covered island like an animal, nearly knocking over the cut eggplant to grab my girlfriend by the throat for an urgent kiss.

She winces and drops the knife to ball a fist into my shirt before breaking out in bubbly giggles. "I could've stabbed you." Her fingers slip through with a fresh slit in the damp fabric, their tips against my already burning skin like salt in a wound. "I have terrible reflexes, and that knife is really sharp."

"And I would let you," I groan against her mouth, using my free hand to lift her by the rounds of that lush ass and latch her strong legs around my hips while stealing another kiss. This woman could stab me, run me over with my truck, and I'd thank her and ask for more.

"Don't tempt me." The warning is playful, but sincere. "I've always been an advocate for women's wrongs. There's a lot of men out there I wanna hurt."

I set her on the back counter, careful that her head doesn't hit the upper cabinets. "You can hurt me instead."

The lightness of the mood lowers, and her flour-dusted palms reach my cheeks. "No." She presses a breathy denial against each of my eyelids. "Never." One of her hands shifts to cover my heart, and its rapid beating takes off with the anticipation of a promise. "I'll never hurt you, Fletcher."

Her molten gaze is the beginning of my end. And I don't care.

"I love you." Bea melts into me, sweeping her parted mouth across mine as I cradle her nape, the dark strands of her hair winding through my fingers and pulling me into their abyss.

"I love you," I echo. "Sleep with me." It's a begged murmur; a prayer left on her lips. It twitches into a faint smile in reply.

"Right now?"

"Yes," I squeeze her soft body to mine, needing to feel every part of her. "Right now. It might kill me if I don't."

"Can't have that." She reaches around the double oven, hitting a button with a beep. "So our dinner doesn't burn."

I nod, still holding onto her.

"Take me to bed, Fletcher." She taps my flexed shoulder twice. "I'm not taking your virginity in the kitchen."

The short route to my bedroom is filled with loving sweeps of touch and impatient, tongue-filled kisses. It's hazy, and I can't tell if it's from the kitchen or from the cloudiness of my own mind.

"Being with you is like walking in a dream," I confess, kneeling at the edge of the bed in front of where I position her. "Please don't wake me up."

"You're everything to me," she answers with an extended kiss to my forehead that leads to her tugging my shirt over my head. The sweat-soaked cotton catches against my beard. I return the favor. She unhooks her bra and drops it onto the floor with a clack. "Everything I ever dreamed of, wished for."

I stare in awe of the absolute goddess, wondering how I became her dream, the object of her affection, desire, her *anything*. A moan escapes me when she pulls down my shorts. I stand, letting them join our clothes on the floor.

She glances ahead at my sheathed cock tenting the boxer briefs, then up at me. "Can I touch you?"

"Please."

Bea gets to her feet, the top of her head reaching my pecs, hot breaths sending wave after wave of goosebumps across my bare torso. I hiss when she strokes my length, struggling to maintain her unrelenting eye contact. My hands curl over the slope of her shoulders, bracing myself at the deliciously slow movements. Tongue peeking from the corner of her mouth, she peels away the briefs from my hips and gapes at how the engorged length slaps against my abs, before testing the weight of me in her shifting clasp.

"You're..." She swallows air, squeezing around me with the next stroke. "I don't know if you'll fit."

I moan in response to her thumbing through the pre-cum beading at the throbbing crown.

"But I wanna try."

Her backward scoot offers the waist of her jeans and has me leaning onto the mattress to strip them from her. Creamy legs cricket together in a *swish* against the duvet, but my hands glide down their firm skin, keeping them apart.

"I've waited for you for so long." I bend to kiss the tops of her feet, the delicate bones of her ankles, up the inside of her knees. She sighs as I continue. "I want to remember...feel everything with you."

It's intoxicating. Her smell, the way her skin tastes, her fingers tangled in my hair, urging my mouth over the curves of her hips and luscious belly. Dusky nipples pucker under my leaden, humid breaths. I lick one, then the other, running on pure instinct while cupping the soft rounds of her breasts.

"I'm living...dying to worship you."

The metal of the piercing clicks against my teeth when I flick my tongue across. I suck until Bea arches from the bed, gushing out my name. My cock leaks against her thigh with a friction-seeking thrust.

"I need you inside me," she pleads, stroking my length and drawing my mouth to hers for a sweltering kiss that nearly has me caving and finishing too quickly.

"Fuck, *please*, gorgeous," I plead back, sounding more desperate than she does. "I wanna give you whatever you want." My lips coast across hers. "Everything you want." I nip into her plump bottom lip, finally fulfilling an earlier fantasy. It's better than I imagined. "But I wanna take my time, fuck you as slowly as possible."

Bea clinches her thighs around my rock-hard length in response, and I bite back a groan. "Don't hold back, Fletcher. Be loud for me."

My hands drop their grip from her tits to the tender flesh of her thighs, spreading her apart while lowering my face into the cleft. "Can I taste you again?"

She nods, mewling. "Yes."

Glistening dark pussy lips wet my beard and mouth, sweet and tart on my tongue, and getting wetter and wetter from each swipe against the soaked flesh. Her fingers dip down to rub the swollen nub, but I move them away, replacing them with my own. My lips rush to her clit to blow a cool breath over its peak. "What about my fingers? You want them, too?"

"Yes," she repeats.

I tease her entrance with a fingertip, and the slick hole allows it to slip in without resistance. "Fuck, you're so wet." I flick my tongue across the clit as my finger curls once, twice, three times against the front wall of her cunt, but it's not enough. I pucker around the raised flesh of her clit before pushing another finger inside her. "Will you come for me?"

Bea responds with a long moan and sucks me in deeper. I shudder into a pause at the heated sensation, balls tightening and cock dripping more sticky pre-cum onto the bed.

"Please, gorgeous? Need you to come before I do."

"Fletcher, yes." The quiet encouragement has my fingers pumping at a relentless pace, then scissoring inside her walls, stretching and curling in sync with the speedy lashes of my tongue on her clit. "*God*, Fletcher."

My name falling from Behraz's lips soothes the pain of her hands tearing at my hair from the scalp, her hips lifting and shifting as she writhes, legs squirming with a judder. "Fletcher, Fletch, fle" —she blubbers— "fle, fl…" until it's only a series of *f-f-f-f*. I imagine she's holding onto the same weak thread of control, as we ready to unravel for each other.

She clamps her thighs around my ears and finishes with a careening cry, body locked in an arch before going limp. I crawl up to cradle her, licking the dripping glaze of her arousal from my lips and leaving behind short, plucky kisses onto her neck, face, and parted mouth. My hands root hers out, lacing our fingers together, eyes wandering all over to take her afterglow in.

"You're even more fucking gorgeous like this, after coming all over my face and fingers." Vision blurry from getting to the edge of pleasure without release, I press my forehead to hers. "I'll never get over it."

One of Bea's hands escapes, skimming down my chest in a sluggish swipe, lower and lower until it wraps the base of my hardened cock. I hurl a grunt in reply, both needing to move and attempting to stay where I am, then peer down, wanting to see myself in her grip. My cock barely fits in her small hand, her fingers and thumb never meeting as she squeezes my impossibly hard erection. I whimper.

"Inside. Now." She lines us up, sweeping me through her soaked cunt and over her clit.

My eyes clench shut, scrambling to move her hand away, and pin it against a pillow. Uneven breaths take over my chest when my hips jolt forward without permission, feeling her wetness, her softness, her warmth across every ridge and snaking vein on the underside of my cock.

"Don't" —I thrust— "rush" —another slow, mind-numbing thrust— "me." All my muscles tense with a shuddering pleasure. "Let me savor you." The head of my cock sits at her core, throbbing, waiting. Her pussy throbs, too.

"Please," she begs, widening her hips with an upward roll.

"Wait." I grab an extra pillow and force it under her ass, angling her bottom half toward me. "I wanna make it good for you."

Bea pulls me to her by the nape, speaking into my mouth, every word breathy and dazed. "Everything you do is good for me." Our sloppy kiss goes tender, and she clings to me, until there's no space, no barrier between us. "I wanna feel everything with you, too." A smile passes between us, eye contact locked. "All of you, Fletcher."

All of me?

Oh.

"No, uh..." What are words? "Condom?"

Her head shakes against mine. "No, only you."

"But—"

"I have an IUD," she murmurs, fingernails digging into the arches of my hips. "Please, Fletcher."

"Fuck, yes." An overeager agreement, surely. But I need her, too. More than I've ever needed anyone or anything. I sidle into her again. "I'll be gentle."

She nods, echoing the sentiment. "Be gentle with me."

The tip of my cock swirls through the wetness, grazing over her clit quickly before settling at the entrance of her perfect cunt. I push in. We gasp. "Fuck."

"Keep going, Fletcher." I drive into her further, letting her relax and accommodate my size. "Little by little, just...like...that."

Every inch is a welcome torture, the stretch of her around me too close to ecstasy. "So fucking snug," I mumble through hurried kisses, a layer of sweat forming between us. "You feel too fucking good, taking it...me so well."

"More," she urges. "Tell me more."

I do, giving her another inch as she clips a moan short. "Like bliss." Her walls pulse and tighten around me, and my head whips back, releasing a feral groan, pleasure ready to spiral free from any restraint. "Fuck, I love you."

"I love you." Bea dotes on my neck, my collarbone. "Need you to move. I'm...so full."

I retreat, then plunge my cock deeper and deeper with each subsequent stride.

"Harder." My body obeys, pliant at her mercy. The next snap of my hips has her feet curling against the backs of my thighs, nails digging into my back.

It's too much, every sensation heightened and barreling me towards a peak of pleasure I didn't know existed. The way she looks beneath me, glowy and unreal. The smell of us, musty and heavy. The taste of her sweet cunt pooling in my mouth. The feel of it, hot and tight and beyond ima-gination.

There's a cliff, and I teeter at its edge, desperate not to fall but knowing a drop is inevitable. "Bea," I moan, my eyes darting in manic lines between hers. "I can't—I'm gonna come."

"Yes." Her hips move in tandem with mine. "Come inside me." She cups my face in her precious hands, slotting our faces together. "Please, Fletcher. Let go."

My thrusts go ragged, sloppy, unable to hold on any longer. And then I rupture into a million pieces, bellowing as if I'm being ripped apart by ecstasy itself, exploding into stars and in a place where time and space don't exist while spilling every shattered shard into the only person who can piece me back together. And she does.

I collapse and she catches me, whispering life into my incapacitated form with praise and awe, adoring me with endless, undeserved kisses and cooling strokes against my heated skin.

"Don't pull out, okay? I wanna feel you a little longer."

I nod with an inhuman grumble, speech beyond my ability in this pivotal moment.

"*Shhh*. You did so good, sweetheart. Fucked me so good."

I don't know how many minutes or hours pass as we lie together, as connected as two people can be, but I don't fight it when she rolls us to our sides to dismount from me. The loss of contact chills me to the bone.

Bea returns with a warm, damp washcloth, wearing my flannel, haphazardly held shut with askew buttons. I hiss and sigh as she cleans the skin between my thighs and groin, and thank God there's no way I could get hard after all that excitement. She rejoins me on the bed, positioning herself parallel to my useless body and playing with the sweat-dampened hair stuck to my forehead. Her sweet face is propped on her elbow when our gazes reconnect.

"Well? Did I kill you?"

I deny it with a smile, shaking my head, despite how full my heart is. "I've never felt more alive."

CHAPTER 24:
THE HOPE OF ACCOMPLISHMENT

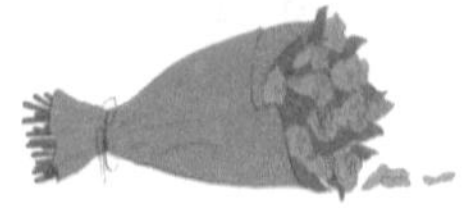

BEHRAZ

August

FLETCHER DONOVAN IS PURE MAGIC.

I know, I know. Logically, I know it's not his cock or mouth that somehow fixed my brain. I know it's the therapy, the curated studying methods, the color-coded tabs to keep important material organized, and of course, it's the accommodations provided to manage my learning disability and ADHD. I know the extended time and frequent breaks will help. But it's also *him*. I memorized so much content because it's in his voice. Its relaxing tone clears my mind of everything else, fading the multitude of noise and static until all that's left is him. And the law, of course.

My attention drops from the folded-over prep manual to a shirtless Fletcher snoozing and curled into my side, arm draped around my belly. He's so fucking beautiful, so serene, so at peace next to me. I never thought I'd bring peace to anyone. He sighs through his nose when my lips skim across his hairline and over his temple. "Sweet man," I coo.

He hums back, content, and sighs again when the capped Sharpie in my hand draws a wayward path up his muscular forearm. Goosebumps appear and disappear from his fair, auburn-speckled skin.

On impulse, I open the permanent marker, wanting to ink him up, connecting those glorious freckles with swirling lines. Lines take shape into leaves and vines, flowers and birds, much like the rich embroidered tapestry on the purple heirloom Gara sari Granny used to wear for Nawroz. Every time she wore it, she reminded us it had been in the family for 250 years.

I don't stop until he stirs with a yawning whine, glancing down at my handiwork.

"What's all this?"

An insecure knot forms in my stomach. "Do you hate it?"

"Are you kidding?" Fletcher sits up, turning his arm to further inspect it. "It's incredible." He brushes away loose ends of my hair from my shoulder, exposing it to push his lips onto my bare skin. "*You're* incredible. In more ways than one."

"Yeah? You think so?"

"If you're asking, I'll have to do better to remind you." Another kiss lands on my jawline, sending a flush over my cheeks. "Smart, sweet, gorgeous, talented. You coulda been an artist."

I scoff. "Nah. My parents thought it was fine, a nice skill to have, but how do you make a living off of doodles?" The manual gets waved in the air. "And now I'm here."

Memories of childhood surge. As the youngest, only daughter of immigrants, I might as well be the eldest. My parents doted on Parvez. He was untouchable, devoid of any responsibilities that ultimately fell on me while they were away. Granny could only do so much, they said. But I was a kid. I deserved to be a kid.

"Hey." Fletcher breaks me from the painful nostalgia, laying a tender stroke to my cheek with the back of his fingers. "Are you nervous for the exam?"

"A little." My phone's alarm rings, signaling I need to get ready. I move to free myself from the lure of staying in bed with my perfect boyfriend, but he pulls me into a fiery kiss, cradling my neck and coaxing me into his lap. The release is too soon.

"Whatever happens" —he crosses the tips of our noses— "I'm so fucking proud of you."

I smile against his mouth, posting my hands on the strong planes of his chest.

"And I'll be there, to bring you home when you're done," Fletcher continues, as if he doesn't realize he's my home more than any place else.

Nerves flutter in my gut as I set my well-organized resources in front of me at the testing center. They ease up when I get through the first multiple-choice section faster than in the past. Skipping the ones I don't know is an effective method, after all. When I return to the questions I couldn't remember off the top of my head, my confidence soars upon efficiently finding the answer. Right when I sense my mind wandering, the proctor announces I have a ten-minute break.

Thank God.

The cycle continues. Every thirty minutes, I step out and walk around, and each time I feel more and more capable of completing this exam within the time given. By the end, I've hit my stride, the routine of short windows of focus and mental rest truly allowing for success. It takes me all day, but it's worth the hope of accomplishment.

Fletcher keeps his promise, waiting outside the examination building in the evening. I get into the truck and gape in surprise at the tray of cupcakes and strawberry smoothie he excitedly holds up.

"For meeee?" I squeal, impatiently removing the tray's lid and biting into the chocolatey frosting without removing the wrapper. "How did you know my blood sugar was dangerously low?"

"Gabe sent the cupcakes." He beams, watching me take a happy gulp from the straw. "But I'll take credit for the smoothie."

"Are you gonna ask me how it went?"

He shakes his head. "I didn't want to be so cliche."

"Oh, who cares? I think it went great," I say through a tired sigh. "I think I could actually pass it this time."

"I think so, too."

"So, what'd you do while I was out?" I peer over with a grateful grin, then pinch my brows together at his shirt, sure that it wasn't the one he wore earlier. "Wait, why're you wearing long sleeves? It's been so warm out, nearly twenty-eight degrees when we took the lunch break."

A wave of red blazes across his face, nearly matching the stoplight we wait at. He tugs his sleeve over his wrist, making a plasticky, crinkling sound. "It's...nothing."

"What'd you do, Fletcher?" Worry takes over when I palm his arm, and he winces. "Did something happen? Tell me you didn't hurt yourself at training."

"I didn't," he denies, suspiciously evading a proper answer. "I'm fine."

"Let me see." Hot tears well at the thought of him in pain. "Please, Fletcher."

He closes his eyes with a strong exhale after we park. "I'll show you. Inside."

I leap from the cab and meet him on the other side, practically dragging him down the hallway to the apartment with the opposite hand from the one he keeps avoiding.

When the door slams behind us, I drop my bag and resort to pleading. "Show me now."

Fletcher's mouth quirks in one corner, backing me onto the sofa before he kneels between my feet. He slips the shirt over his head in one easy swoop, and I almost get distracted by how stunning he is before noticing the clear cling wrap on his arm and recognizing what's underneath: an outline of the large pattern I drew on him earlier.

"It's" —my fingers coast over the plastic, retracing the lines, the pulse at his wrist beating rapidly under my touch— "you..." I can't help but whisper. "You got it tattooed."

"It's permanent, yeah." Confidence and pride lace his tone. "It was too beautiful not to keep forever." Happiness rolls through my chest, saltwater stinging my eyes, and I wonder if he meant the design or me. "I have a second session to fill it in. You like it?" He lifts my hands to flank his face. "Tell me you like it."

"I love it." I nod, moving my thumbs and fingers through the soft, tidy facial hair. "And I love you."

"I love you, Behraz." His gaze fixes on mine, sparkling with pure devotion. "I want my days to start and end with you. And anytime I can't, at least now I can look down and have a piece of you with me."

CHAPTER 25:
YOU'RE ALL OF MY DREAMS COMING TRUE

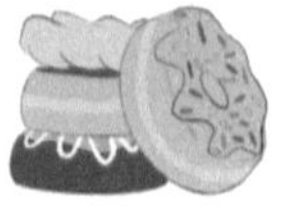

FLETCHER

TWO MONTHS WITH BEHRAZ IRANI ISN'T NEARLY enough.

The calendar taunts that horrible, giant red circle around the date, glaring at me from the side of the fridge where it hangs. I'm tempted to hide it. Maybe if she doesn't see it, she won't remember.

I bolt over there to rip it from its place and toss it into the recycling bin, mixing it with some fliers and bills from the mailbox. The trash drawer closes without a sound, and I fold my torso over the island counter until my forehead meets the granite. I encase my pathetic face with both arms, the cool surface doing nothing to alleviate the blood surging nervously through me. Remembering the night before only worsens it.

Behraz pushed me into a reclined position before thumbing over the crown of my upright cock, red and angry, shiny and dribbling pre-cum down its length. "Love when you're so desperate for me, Fletcher," she purred, her voice low and honeyed. "Makes me feel so fucking hot."

"You are, Bea." I couldn't think of anything but her. "So hot."

She moaned at the compliment, sliding over my slick cock with her naked cunt, sandwiching it between her flesh and my lower belly, but not pushing inside. The teasing, fuck, the teasing would finish me off too quick. My first time with her on top and I wasn't sure if she was edging me or herself. One palm posted onto my chest; Bea used her free hand to fist my cock and position it where she wanted.

"Bea," I begged, hot need and desire taking over.

She inserted my cock into the glossy flesh with a soft simper, and I nearly blacked out from watching more of it disappear in her cunt. Something rumbled from deep within me.

"Do you like this?" she asked, her ragged breaths mirroring mine.

"Yes." I clutched her lush thighs, her generous hips, leashing something beastly within me, wanting her to maintain control, wanting her to use me, use me to come.

She glided off, only to press her knees to my sides and take more of me. "Say it."

"I...like it," —I struggled to find words that weren't yes or her name— "I like when you ride me."

"Yeah? What else?" She impaled herself again, soaking my cock further with her arousal. "When you talk, I can't hear myself think. Which is perfect, Fletcher, because my mind never shuts up. Keep talking."

"You...Bea. God."

"Yes, it's me, sweetheart. Keep going." Her head lolls back, tickling my thighs with the ends of her hair, grinding against me. "Tell me how it feels. How much you love it." Her hips rolled and rolled, their pace becoming torturous.

"You're my paradise," I groaned, scrambling together thoughts at her demand. "Fucking love how rosy you get—your cheeks, your lips, your nipples" —I paused my grunting to crush her breast in one palm— "your cunt. All dark, wet, tight for me."

"Fletcher," she moaned again, keening at a higher pitch than her natural tone. "Hold on to me. Fuck me from below."

I did, grabbing her ass and thrusting from below with an unyielding speed, losing my fucking mind at the way her breasts bounced. "I'm so... unbelievably hard, Bea. I'm gonna come inside you." My girlfriend only moaned in reply, open-mouthed, every inch of her skin covered in a pink blush. "Can I? Or do you want me to come on your perfect tits again?"

"Inside...I'm right there, so close," she whined, moving her cunt in insane circles while I was still deep inside her. "Fletcher."

"Fuck, my heart might give out," I confessed, pulse rattling in my *throat. "The fact that you're sitting on my cock—" I groan loudly. "But I don't want to stop, Bea."*

For the record, if this is how I'd go, it'd be worth it.

Her knees drew apart, sucking my cock in until I buried fully within her pussy. The harsh movement elicited another extended moan from me, the vibrations stilling Behraz in an arch as she finished with a series of shudders and igniting my own orgasm until she and I burned and burned.

Mind and cock emptied, I rolled us until she was on her back, staying pulsing inside her and pressing my weight onto her. We shared dazed giggles and ardent kisses, twining our fingers together.

"You're a dream, Behraz." I pecked all over her sweet face, the delicate skin of her neck. "You're all of my dreams coming true."

I scrub my face and tug at my cock as I stand, trying to rid myself of the memory and a raging boner, but it doesn't stop the tears.

I'm a fucking idiot. To think I could live with Behraz and not fall in love with her to the point of breaking, to love her so deeply that it ruined me for everyone else. I'll never love anyone like her, and I don't want to, either. My knees buckle by the sofa, and I fall to the cushions, sobbing into my hands and yanking my hair until my scalp goes numb. What if she wants to go? I can't trap her. I won't trap her. Good, I'll just die instead. Perfect plan, Fletch. Well-thought-out. I sniffle loudly.

"Oh, my God, Fletcher." Bea's touch rouses me from the pathetic display. I didn't even hear her come in over my own sniveling. "What's wrong, sweetheart?" She wipes tear stains from my cheeks with her lips.

"I" —my lips suck in short breaths— "don't want" —I try to reel in the sobbing— "you to go."

She huffs out a quick laugh through her concerned smile. "Where am I going exactly?"

"Moving...out." I gasp twice. "Don't."

"Fletcher."

My head shakes side to side, inconsolable and weeping. "How am I supposed to move on after this? It's like my dreams came true, but now they're ending." Bea shushes me, but I keep blubbering. "Am I expected to survive the end? Because it feels like I'm dying."

"I mean, we said two months, but—"

"I don't care what we said," I pout. "I don't want you to go."

She smiles, wide and bright. How can she smile at a time like this? "You want me to stay?"

"Yes."

Bea hums, twisting her mouth to one side. "For how long?"

I sniffle again, then wipe it with the bottom of my shirt. "Is forever okay?"

"That's funny," she says, tipping my chin up to hers until our lips align. "That's precisely how long I was planning to be here."

CHAPTER 26:
GAME'S NOT OVER YET

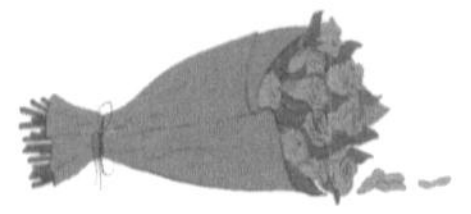

BEHRAZ

"I DON'T LIKE SURPRISES."

Scolding my boyfriend seems ungrateful, but I don't mean to be. Whatever he's done for me, everything he continues to do for me? It's more than I could expect from anyone.

"Especially when I don't know where I'm going," I add, tapping on the smooth blindfold. "This thing is for the bedroom only."

"There's time for that yet, gorgeous." The husky murmur sends electric excitement down my spine.

"Promise?"

"Promise," he confirms, curling our pinkies together. Fletcher positions me in the opposite direction. "Ready?"

"As I'll ever be."

He loosens the secure knot tied over my ponytail, enough so the loop of fabric pools around my neck.

A rose gold Audi SUV topped with a giant matching bow sits in a parking spot next to Fletcher's truck. My mouth parts. "You...bought me a car?"

"I saw it and thought of you." His smile splits free as his hand captures mine. "You like it, right?"

The man bought me a fucking car. And a pricey one at that. "Fletcher, it's too much."

"Whaddya mean?" He cocoons me in his strong arms. "Too flashy? Too pink?"

"And too expensive. I won't be able to pay you back for it."

Fletcher clicks his tongue and pelts the end of my nose with a kiss. "That's why it's called a gift."

I make a disapproving noise, vocalizing my grievances while he physically sways me, as if the motion will convince me to accept this lavish present.

"Come on, you need it."

"I don't." Another car would have done just fine, but no. This man had to go and get a char char bangadi wali gadi, as my mom says. *She* would be thrilled with its luxury. I feel spoiled and unworthy. "You could've bought a new truck."

"Mine works fine. *You* passed the bar, gorgeous. You deserve it." His hands wind together at the small of my back, swishing around the chiffon fabric of my sundress. "What, you were going to ride your bike to the office? Not on my watch," he says with a finality. "I can't have the next big name in international law show up to court with some shoddy heap of junk." Fletcher hooks my hands around his neck, and I have to lift my feet until I'm on the tips of my toes. "Plus, I won't be around during the regular season to drive you, or else you know I would."

Funnily enough, I won't be either.

"About that." I draw my gaze up to his. It's so molten and adoring, I hope what I divulge next doesn't ruin it. "Remember the interview Dr. Ahmad set up for me? For the apprenticeship?"

"Mmhmm," he replies hazily, distracting me with the taste of his lips.

The distraction is working. "I...got it."

"Amazing," Fletcher gushes, his sweet praise bittering the news.

"It starts" —I can hardly piece together the sentence from the way his mouth and tongue ravish a sensitive spot below my ear— "in January."

"Perfect."

I gasp when the delicate skin along my neck gets pulled between his teeth. "It's in London."

He freezes, then eases his hold on me. "London?"

I nod, swallowing a hesitant gulp, wholly unsure of how this will change us.

"Like, across the ocean, in a different country, London?"

"Yeah."

"Fuck, Bea." Our foreheads fall to one another as we puff out a synchronous breath. "I hate this." My heart cracks at the disappointed whisper. "But you gotta go."

"I do?"

His head moves up and down, forcing mine to nod, too. "You've worked too fucking hard."

"What about..." The lump lodged in my throat robs me of any eloquence. "You...us?"

"I'll be here," he confirms. "I'm not going anywhere."

"What if—"

Fletcher places a finger over my mouth. "I've waited for you for six years, Behraz. What's six months?"

Nothing makes sense but the weepy *I love you's* I murmur into his skin.

"I love you, too." Fletcher brushes tears from my cheeks with his thumbs, kissing my face all over. "Let's take your new car for a ride, hey?" He hands over the keyless remote, unlocking it with a beep before tugging at the black knot around my throat until it steals my breath. "Then we can take this blindfold for a ride."

"Can we...record it?" I ask sweetly. "For days you're on the road?"

"Abso-fucking-lutely."

———

I don't think this is what he had in mind when he wanted to use the blindfold, but here we are. His agreement was, shall we say, *enthusiastic*.

You can do whatever you want to me, he said, *anything and everything*.

My attention switches between the makeshift phone camera on the tripod and the black silk ribbon cutting through the stunning red waves of hair atop his head. The sight of the rest of him? Goddamn.

Fletcher Donovan lies on his mattress, clothed in nothing but his bare, peachy skin and the network of freckles, wrists bound above his head with a shiny, self-sticking tape. Both arms extend fully as they hang off a screwed-in hook atop the tufted headboard. Similar hooks chained to leather straps attached to his ankles keep his bottom half spread-eagled.

Heavy desire heats me from the inside, throbbing low in my core until my pulse beats through every layer of my body. I strip, clammy skin already making it difficult to remove the lightweight dress.

"Bea?" he calls toward the window, in the opposite direction from where I stand in nothing but a sheer black bra and thong. "Where are you?"

I answer with a feathery touch to the soles of his feet. "Right here." He tips up his chin with a short intake of air, his toes curling in response. "Can you see anything?"

His light pink tongue licks the seam of his lips, as if able to taste me. "Only you."

There's no physical response to me waving a hand in front of his covered eyes. "Are you sure?"

"I don't need my vision to see you, Bea. I see you all the time in my mind. Even when you're not here. I close my eyes, and there you are. Feeling real as right now, the most beautiful creature I've ever laid eyes on."

I suddenly get the appeal of all those romantasy books he loves. His praise wets the strip of thong on my pussy, leaking my arousal onto my inner thighs. "When do you think of me?"

"All the time. All the fucking time." He breathes out the second sentence, seemingly pained and relieved at the same time. "Every time I touched myself...held my cock for the past six years."

Heat courses downward. Being nearly naked isn't helping after all. I free my chest from the cage of the bra, then tuck my fingers below the strings of fabric on each hip, stretching them. "Can you see me now?"

"Yes," he gasps, perking an ear. "You're...taking off your...clothes." Fletcher's body tenses, skin staked with goosebumps, his pink nipples pebbling into hard peaks when my thong pools to the floor. My palms cover my breasts with a harsh squeeze. He hisses. "You're touching your... tits." I strum my fingers over my nipples in a few circles, relishing the combined attention from his words and my own touch. "Fuck."

One of my hands descends further down my midsection, skimming past my belly button, two fingers dipping into the slick cleft of my pussy. The other hand stays on my chest, gently pinching the nipple's piercing. "And now?"

His hips jolt up, swollen cock slapping against his defined abs as he tightens.

"Oh, my *fuck*," he strangles out a tortured noise when I swipe through my cunt, needy and pulsing. "I can hear...how wet you are." Pre-cum streaks across the muscles of his stomach and drips through his happy trail.

I raise my arousal-coated fingers to my line of sight, smirking at a fresh idea. "Wanna play a game with me, Fletcher?"

Fletcher nods, rapid and overeager. "Yes."

My knees hike up to join him on the mattress, climbing until I straddle his toned torso. "I'm gonna put something in your mouth." His cock bounces. "You have to guess what it is." The broad squares of his chest heave.

"If you guess right, you get to taste the next thing."

"Okay."

I stifle laughter by puffing my mouth, leaning forward to offer my elbow to Fletcher's parted lips. He accepts with a hungry suck, and I break with a giggle.

"Elbow."

My face angles to his, inhaling the humid air from his ragged breaths. I offer my lips next, lightly pressing them over his. He latches on with a wince, swiping his tongue against mine in quick lashes. I pull away with a wide smile.

"Your perfect fucking mouth."

"Stick out your tongue," I direct. He does. Both glazed fingers land on the flattened muscle, and he draws them in, suctioning and licking them clean, releasing a heady moan when I retract them. I tsk. "That's not an answer."

"You," he chokes, "your wetness."

"Good boy."

While he stammers nonsense at the simple praise, I savor the control, the feeling of power over him. Retrieving more of the fluid from between my legs, I bite back a pleasured sound when spreading it over my nipple, then bend to hover over his open, waiting mouth.

He suckles, even hungrier, needier than before, his deep grumble vibrating deliciously through my breast as the hairs of his beard tickle its delicate skin.

I gasp. "Fletcher."

"*Fuck*, you're killing me," he groans, words mashing together in a desperate mumble. "Sit on my fucking face already."

"Ah, ah, ah." The admonishment has his chin quivering. "Game's not over yet." My gaze reaches the chef's knife resting on the nightstand, and my hand follows. The metallic hiss from a sole finger sliding across the broad blade's spine seems to have the same effect on Fletcher. I rest it against his lips, silencing him for a moment before commanding him further. "Taste." I scrape it gently across his bearded jaw and down his pretty, blushing throat. "What is it?"

A knot of raised tendon glides up and down the column of his neck. The pink tinting his skin reddens. "A knife."

"Should I keep going?"

"*Please.*"

My heart thumps manically, measuring each reaction to the back of the blade dragging down his chest. A line across his collarbone has his nostrils flaring.

"Fu-f-*fuuuuck.*"

He whimpers when I flick the knife's blunt edge over a pursed nipple, then lick and suck to lessen the sting. The repeated treatment on the other side elicits yet another whimper, strings of more pre-cum making a beautiful mess on his stomach. Sinews in his wrists and forearms strain against his bind as I continue, alternating a squiggling path of blade and nibbles through the muscles of his abdomen with the tip, careful not to nick or break the skin.

I take the blade between my clenched teeth, relishing the cold metal against my tongue before posting my hands into his chest. My body slides down, then straightens to see the result: gorgeous freckles dotting peachy skin, mottled in red lines and bite marks.

"Look at how shtunning you are," I gush. "Worked yourself up into a filthy mess."

"Please, Bea." His plea is barely a whisper, and I grip his cock, positioning myself with a snake-like slither over the length without allowing entrance. He lets out a strangled simper. "Fuck me."

I grind into it again and again, teasing myself until our moans blend.

"You like that?" His hips thrust, slipping the engorged crown of his cock over my clit with an unbelievable pressure. "You like soaking my cock with all that sweetness?"

My agreeing hum vibrates through the steel of the blade. I rock over him again.

"You like tormenting me?"

I confirm with another pleasured noise.

"'Cause I fucking love it, Bea." Fletcher gasps, the muscles on his hips flexing and showing off their perfect *v*. "I'm gonna come."

I spit the knife and catch the black handle in my palm. "Not yet," I say over the knife, lowering to remove myself and flanking the thick flesh of his thighs with my knees. Catching a glimpse of his tightened balls distracts me momentarily, and I bend to circle one with my tongue, then the other, the velvety skin starting to glisten with my spit. I mouth them and release when I gag, remembering my task and the object in hand.

The weighted handle warms in my grasp. I flip it a few times. Finally, the blunt spine meets his hardened cock, and I draw a line on the underside from the root, over the ridges and throbbing veins, and past the apex of his leaking slit. His hands turn to white fists, another tortured, guttural sound bellowing from him before I discard the knife onto the nightstand and clamber over him, the anticipation weakening my resolve by the minute.

"Bea," he says through a needy whimper. "*Goddamn it*, fuck me already."

I brace my hands against his chest once more. The smallest insertion of just the tip stretches me, and we both quickly suck in a gulp of air at the sensation.

"M-more," he begs, hips tilting up, "need...to feel more...of you."

My arms shake, my thighs shake, *hell*, my pussy shakes while taking his girth. It's not possible for him to somehow be bigger than the last time, right? This is what you get for falling in love with a kinky, monster-dicked hockey player, Behraz. You've made this your cock, and now you have to sit on it. I switch the angle to slide down further, take him deeper. When I adjust and throw my hips back, Fletcher snaps like a whip, unintentionally driving his cock deep into me. It's a harsh and sudden motion, and my mouth locks open with a shuddering moan.

"I know, gorgeous," he grits through his teeth, "I *know*. It hurts. But you're gonna make that tight cunt of yours take it all, aren't you?"

"Yes." It's the only word I can remember right now. "Yes," I repeat, getting into a rhythm. The slapping of my ass onto his hips is enough to drive anyone insane, but watching our bodies fuse is ethereal. And seeing how it cuts every flimsy thread of Fletcher Donovan's restraint one by one is nothing short of a drug-addled ecstasy. I relish it, my eyes stretching as if trying to take in more of the moment, drunk with power and aching for an end to this torture.

The tandem orgasm reaches a precipice, each of our mixed moans and mewls and groans and screaming, flying by the point of no return. My vision goes white, starry in a flash of pleasured bliss.

There's a stutter of his hips, the last rung of control cracking beneath me. The manic, uneven thrusts end as my walls clench, and I shiver through the high. He stills with a jolt, bowing off the bed as he releases warm cum into the deepest part of me, so full of his cock, nothing escapes.

Our sweaty bodies collide as I collapse into a heap onto his chest, softening cock still pulsing inside me. We share a crazed, satisfied giggle, heaving under the combined weight of our slowing breaths.

I raise my head to his blinded form and admire his persistent blush through the fog of the aftermath. Pretty freckles start reappearing from the strong pink hue. Goosebumps rise in the wake of my touch across his heated skin. "What do you feel?"

"You." Fletcher returns a nearly inaudible rasp.

"Where?"

"Everywhere."

His obsession is intoxicating, and I can't help enabling it. "One last taste, then?" Questioning eyebrows wrinkle his forehead above the blindfold. "Yes or no?"

"Yes." Maybe that's the only word left in his brain, too.

I muster up the last of my energy and straighten, lifting myself from his lifeless cock. We both sigh, but his breath ends in a choked gargle when my knees settle on either side of his face, hands curling over the top of the headboard. I relax the muscles of my core, spilling out a string of his cum. It lands on the perfect, pink seam of his lips and drips onto his inviting tongue.

Fletcher trembles, an aftershock of tension bursting across his body, and I lower, suffocating him with my cunt. He gorges on me, mouthing and licking and sucking until he's left whimpering, simpering from desperation. The relentless devouring overwhelms me, and a secondary orgasm rockets through at lightspeed.

One set of my fingers comb through his damp hair, pulling the silk from his eyes so he can see the mess he's made. They roll as he swallows with a satisfied rumble, and stay shut as I reposition, shifting to lick our mixed release from his ruddy cheeks and facial hair.

"Us," he mumbles through a sigh, answering an unasked question. "We taste so fucking good."

I chuckle, going lax post-orgasm. "You win." My head lolls to my shoulder, allowing a hazy peek at Fletcher's limp cock, flopped over and stuck to his thigh with a sheen of our cum.

It's dead. I've managed to kill it. Poor guy can't even leak anymore.

I can't free Fletcher fast enough, undoing the ankle straps and using the knife to clip to the tape circling his wrists. He tears from the bind and in the next blink, I'm on my back, savoring the delicious weight of his leaden, muscled body.

"Two...minutes," he pants between breathy kisses. His hands wander, roughly squeezing my breasts, my waist, my hips, my thighs. "Gimme two minutes. Then you're gonna turn around and get back on this cock so I can look at your perfect ass while I fuck you into next week."

———

The following morning is lazy.

I float in and out of consciousness, the only constants Fletcher Donovan's thrumming heartbeat and his gentle touch. When I finally wake, I'm sprawled out on my front, tits pressed into his abs and my lower half outlined by his legs. The drape of a soft cotton sheet covers me, cooling me as I stretch my feet and frou-frou between the wrinkles. His fingers lace hypnotic swirls through the tangled mess of my hair. My head angles up from the valley of his chest, the view so spectacular, it's almost unreal. But it isn't.

It's real. He's real, exposed, and naked as I am, propped up on the headboard, his free hand holding an open book toward the light from the window.

"Morning, gorgeous," he greets through an innocent, lopsided smile. As if we didn't rail each other up the stairway to heaven and back into the early hours of the day. Warm lips paint a kiss onto my forehead. The dark line of his lashes flutters, batting at me with an adoring look. Like all he wants to look at is me. The warmth of our cocoon spreads, filling my chest.

And because I'm not normal, I can't even say good morning back. "Fletcher? Why do you love me?"

"Hmm?" A dazed reply. His fingers relent from their luscious pressure on my scalp and dote on my cheeks and chin with feathery light sweeps. "Yes, I do love you."

"Why?"

Fletcher narrows his eyes, still smiling. "Because you're my joy, Bea. You're my sunshine on cloudy days."

Bum, bum-bum-bum-bum, bum...My mind scats along to the Temptations classic, "My Girl," and I have to really rein it in so I don't get carried away and belt out the lyrics.

Fletcher's thumb grazes over my lips. "When you smile, every worry, every chest-tightening pressure of my anxiety melts away." My closed mouth stretches at his praise. "Yeah, just like that." I beam, crinkling my nose. "And you're warm."

"Oh! Sorry." An attempt is made to detach from where our skin connects. "I know I'm sweaty from tossing and turning—"

Fletcher doesn't let me go. "Not like that. You're accepting, welcoming. Patient."

"Me?" I toss my head back to cackle. "Patient? I don't have a patient cell in my body."

He shakes out a denial. "You're patient with me."

My finger boops the adorable tip of his nose. "I could say the same thing about you." A feeling of shame has my eyes averting downward. "I know I'm not easy to deal with..."

"Deal with? Bea..." he intones, placing his book on the bedside table before hoisting me up to a seated straddle. "Come here." Both hands hold my face, forcing my gaze to his. "You're perfect for me." One kiss dots my cheek. "Nothing about you is a burden." Another kiss dots the opposite cheek. "I chose you—I'm choosing you. All of you." His lips find a sweet spot on my neck. "Chaos, chattiness, unhinged thoughts, everything. I'll choose you over anyone else, every time." A final kiss to the space over my heart has it fluttering in its cage. "Okay?"

I nod, too overcome with his devotion to say anything, and return my head to his chest. Fletcher sighs and picks up his book again, but my mind is restless, spinning all the worst-case scenarios, all the ways this could fall apart, as any good thing in my life inevitably does.

"Fletcher?"

"Yeah, sweetheart?"

"Do you want kids?"

"I don't know." He barely glances from the page he's on.

"Would you...still love me if I didn't want them?" My eyes clench, bracing for an unfavorable answer.

"Of course," he says, mindless and unfazed. "Love isn't conditional, Bea."

"'Cause I think I'd be a terrible mother."

Fletcher drops his book and exhales through his nose. "I don't believe that for a second."

"And anyway," I continue the argument, though there's clearly none to be had, "I don't want things to change, like, ever. I like our little life. I don't want to share you. Is that selfish?"

"It's not selfish," he practically coos. "Do you know how many children are born for selfish reasons? I'm happy with you. You're more than enough for me."

My smile widens maniacally at the assurance.

"And if we wanna be around some tiny humans, I'm sure our friends or my siblings will be glad to let us spend time with theirs."

"Okay." I toy nervously with the short hairs between his pecs. "You don't think you'd get bored?"

"Of what?"

This man really doesn't find me boring or annoying at all? I am horribly annoyed by the idea.

"Me!" My arms shoot up, exasperated. "A whole life of only ever kissing *me*, sleeping with *me*, only being with *me*. Wouldn't you find it absolutely, completely, *unbearably* boring?"

Fletcher laughs from his belly, the rare sound deep and glorious and jiggling all my lumpy bits. "A whole life with just you, boring? No, not a chance." His hands gather the loose hairs cascading over my shoulders and upper back, drawing our faces together. "That's my dream." The husky whisper across my lips is better than any vow. "Tell me I'm lucky enough for the rest of my dreams to come true, Bea. I only wanna be with you."

CHAPTER 27:
THEY'RE NOT THE BOSS OF YOU, I AM

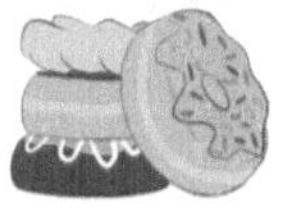

FLETCHER

October

THE THOUGHT OF BEHRAZ IRANI IS RUINOUS.

From the moment I wake to when I lie to rest for the night, I feel her on every square inch of my skin. She doesn't need to be physically there. Each spark lit by my functional neurons fires her name. She's so deeply embedded in my soul that if death tried to part us, it'd have to take me with it. And I wouldn't have it any other way. I'll live and die for this woman.

Behraz kisses the inside of my wrist across the cab of my truck. Her lips nip over the vein, drumming up excitement in my pulse. I shudder. "We're gonna get into an accident."

She nods and *mmm*s but doesn't stop. "I can't help it." Her lips cinch around my skin, and my shoulder lifts, rolling a shiver down to the tips of my fingers. "You're just so...cute and nibble-able."

Pins and needles prickle up the same arm, and my warning comes out more like a plea for mercy. "Bea."

"Pull over, Dreamboat."

As if I'd ever say no to her. I throw on the hazards and park next to the highway, the roads nearly empty from the early hour.

Her seatbelt releases with a click, and her hand stays clasped to mine as she bends a knee onto the leather seat and faces me. "Fletcher."

I stare ahead, afraid of falling apart. Even before the tender contact, I'd been distracted on the drive to the airport. Miller convinced me to come home for Thanksgiving, using Dad's retirement and ailing health, and citing the stretch of time since my last visit.

"You should," Bea said once I got off the phone with my sister. Leaden guilt pressed into my chest. Her head tilted toward me in comfort and understanding, the sweep of her hand over the slope of my shoulders softening the weight held there. "It's family."

"You're my family." My lips reached for her temple, cherishing its soft warmth.

"I know," she cooed, "You're my family too, but if you want and it helps, I'll come along."

I agreed. I'd go anywhere with her.

"Fletcher, look at me."

When I don't, she raises the console and climbs onto my lap, positioning my arms tight around her hips and cupping my face in her sweet hands. If she thinks this is a punishment, joke's on her. This is exactly where I wanna be.

"I'm here, okay?" A wrinkle forms in my brow when our foreheads meet. I inhale her, her chaotic energy now a familiar calm. "Don't think I haven't noticed you've been uneasy this past week."

Everything with my family makes me uneasy. Everything is overcomplicated. Meals, sleeping arrangements, *fuck*, the sheer number of people and the expected onslaught of comments about contracts and questions about the future of my career have my anxiety ready to flood out.

Instead, I dam it, burying my face in the crook of her neck, wanting to drown in rosewater and never come up for air. Her heavy sigh pushes our chests together. "What's going on in that *outrageously* handsome head of yours?"

That cracks open my smile, widening against her skin, and she must feel it because she hums in approval.

"There it is."

I knock my head into the headrest with a sharp, whiny exhale. "I don't wanna face them. It's always...too much." My palms are sweaty just thinking about it. "The noise, the constant talking, arguing, kids screaming, *God*..." The overstimulation requires many days of solitude afterward. I let her go to scrub my face with both hands, surely leaving behind a red hue.

Her expression shifts, puzzled at the admission. "What do you do when you're on the ice? How do you block the noise out?"

"That's different." My fingers scratch a spot behind my ear. "There's separation. They're behind the boards, and they're strangers. I can drown them out."

"You get into the so-called 'zone?'"

"Yeah. And while I wish I could, I can't really tune out my family."

"Good thing I'm chatty and charming," Bea's shoulder lifts, eyes rounding, playful and coy. "I can field all the small talk."

What a horrible job. My sisters are fine, if not overbearing in a well-intentioned way, but a cardboard cutout makes a more interesting conversation partner than Parker.

"That's the other thing: bringing you into their wreckage. They don't..." —one eye wrinkles shut in a cringe— "see me like you do." I don't want her to see the way they treat me. "I don't want it to change what you think of me, I guess..."

"Nothing can change that." Her palms slide to my chest, over the pumping organ that beats only for her. "I know, see, feel who you are. You're my boyfriend. My Dreamboat. What they say doesn't matter to me."

"But—"

"*Shh.*" The hush of her breath draws a long, shaky breath from me, neck going lax from the massaged circles into my nape. "We don't have to stay, okay? If you're not having a good time, we can visit for a bit and spend the night somewhere else. You can even blame it on me."

I nod loosely. "Okay."

Bea scoots from my lap but keeps one set of our hands entwined. "Now," she begins, wearing a naughty grin, "are you ready to drive to the airport or would you rather me suck the life out of your cock so we can have a relaxed flight?"

———

When we get to Charlottetown, I detour onto Route 1, driving the rental Chevy on the scenic way to Summerside. And it's so worth it.

Bea's smiles and excited giggles quite literally clear the rainclouds from the shore. It lightens the worry on my face, too, and I loosen my shoulders, relaxing into my seat.

I don't recall appreciating the foamy surf smacking against those magnificent red cliffs, the rolling green hills in the distance, for a long time. Maybe since I was a kid. Once I left, the lush island's scenery was a reminder of weighty responsibilities rather than a thing of beauty. Perspective is funny like that.

Behraz makes everything wondrous and joyful. I'll never get over having her by my side.

"I feel like I'm in Green Gables!" Her arms stretch over her head before she bunches one sleeve of her sweater to her elbow, then lowers the window to stick a hand out, moving her palm like a wave through the cool airstream. Dark strands whip across her cheeks, getting tangled in her eyelashes. "You're totally Gilbert Blythe." When the waves ebb into the ocean, the wind rustles the leaves.

"Oh, yeah?" Wait until she hears my family's favorite nickname for me.

She returns a single enthusiastic nod. "He was my very first book boyfriend."

"Typically, I'd be very jealous of that esteemed position," I tease, my hand squeezing the soft flesh of her upper thigh. "But he's fictional, and I'm not."

"I like when you're like this," she snaps back. "Makes it more fun to fuck the sass right out of your pretty mouth."

I choke on my own spit, the heated blood from a fiery blush searing the surfaces of my neck and face. And much lower. "Please, gorgeous." The side of my fist knocks some clarity into my throat. "If I show up at home as hard as I am now, I'll never be able to live it down."

Almost an hour later, we pass Chelton Beach. "It's a red sand beach!" Bea *ooh*s and *aah*s. "And the blue picnic benches?" She swoons against the truck door. "You literally grew up in the cutest place ever."

I point ahead, through the windshield, at a cluster of tall trees beyond the grass edging the sandbars. "That's where I'd end up after about twenty minutes. In the shade. Sunscreen and a rash guard weren't enough." I shake my head through a half-smile at the countless visits spent sunburnt—*or trying not to be*—at the beach. "My sisters would run around the shoreline, alternating between sunbathing, hitting a volleyball back and forth, and going for a swim. Parker would pop open a couple of nets and shake a couple sticks overhead, yelling at me to play him in beach hockey."

A chuckle vibrates at the base of my throat. "I'd pretend not to hear him and hide behind *A Wrinkle in Time* or *The Giver* or whatever I had picked up from the library that week. Or I'd lie and say Piper told me to watch Harper and Hunter make sandcastles." My smile widens at the memories. Life here wasn't all bad. "Then Mom would show up after her shift with juice boxes and start an assembly line to have us make peanut butter and jelly sandwiches for dinner."

She sucks in a whistled breath through pursed lips. "Sounds better than summers with my granny quizzing me on multiplication tables or listening to her make politically incorrect and borderline racist comments about our neighbors." Behraz shoots me a mischievous smile. "When she dozed off on the couch, I'd steal strawberry hard candies from her purse. I thought I was so sly, but she always knew."

I slow the engine when turning onto the street where my parents live.

Bea gasps. "This is beautiful, Fletch. This is your childhood home?"

"Nah, I bought it for them as a rookie." I was worth more than I am now, fresh out of the juniors. The team had high hopes, I guess.

The historic, Craftsman-style house sits in the heart of Summerside, slate grey paint keeping up from last year when I got the exterior done. "It's walkable to the pier and to Mom's store, plus it's got six bedrooms, which is hard to come by unless you do a custom build."

We pull into the long driveway that ends in a detached two-car garage. There are already three vans and two cars parked, which means I'm the last of my siblings to arrive.

"This is all you, huh?" Bea's mouth wrinkles in one corner. "You're a really good son, you know that?"

I turn to squint at the wraparound porch, stalling. "Not sure they'd agree."

"Well, they're not the boss of you." Her pointer finger wags in the direction of the house, then jabs into her sternum. "*I* am." There's not a trace of joking in her tone, but I can't help but smile. She harrumphs. "And *I* say let's go inside and set them straight."

Bea mutters to herself as we walk up. "Piper, Parker, Greer, Miller..." She clicks her tongue after a pause, then repeats it. "Piper, Parker, Greer, Miller...?"

"Harper and Hunter. But they aren't here anyway. I don't expect you to—"

I've lost her. Her ranty train of thought cannot be stopped.

"Peter Piper picked a peck of pickled peppers," she adds with a mumbled curse. "Fall in love with a Peter and his giant pecker and face the whole peck of Peters, eldest sister Piper."

I snort. "Bea, what are you doing?"

"Trying to keep track of all your siblings' names without getting tongue twisted. It's nerve-wracking."

"My older sisters are...something." Hell, I'm nervous, too. "And everyone gets them mixed up. It's fine. But you gotta stop talking about my" —I motion to my groin with my eyes— "pecker."

"Right." She closes her eyes and shakes the idea away. "If I talk about it, it'll wake up and want to play."

My cock twitches. God damn it.

"Bea, please." We're having a hard time staying serious, both tearing into goofy smiles like a couple of idiots in love. "I'm begging you."

"You know how that's my favorite."

The playful mood drops when I push open the front door, giving way to a violent pile of footwear in the entryway: all various shapes, sizes, and colors. And it's not only the kids who are to blame. Half a dozen adult pairs are strewn amongst them. Only a couple of pairs line up with their twin on the opposite side. Probably an effort by Piper and Miller, the only organized women to ever come through this house.

If someone walked in without looking, they'd trip over the ludicrous number of shoes, fall headfirst onto the floor, and die on the spot. I make sure that isn't Behraz's fate, guiding her by the hand as we traverse the uneven terrain and leave our shoes next to my sisters' neatened sets.

Muted squeals and the laughter of children sound out from the yard as she inspects the solid woodwork of the banister with a sweep of her hand. Her eyes twinkle at the light shining through the stained glass window on the landing. A soft awe sweetens her tone. "So pretty."

There's a scuffle coming our way when the heavy wooden door slams behind us. A gaggle of my older sisters and their husbands halt their stampede and gape at us, then at our held hands, then between me and Bea. Blood rises from my chest with a fury, tinging my neck and face with red. She squeezes the hold.

"Holy shit." Lucas blinks three times, like a cartoon. Greer elbows him.

For a pair of English teachers, they're suddenly lost for words.

"Pipe!" Dylan calls over his shoulder without breaking his eye contact. Piper is the only one missing. "Look what the cat dragged in."

Bea mutters under her breath, speaking into my arm. "Am I the cat or you?"

My oldest sister rounds the corner from the kitchen in the back, coffee mug in hand, and sees me first. "*Aw*, hey, Annie! You made it." She joins the frozen group when she notices my plus-one.

"Annie?" Bea's voice is no longer at a whisper.

A dozen questioning eyes fall back to her, then to me.

"Anne brought a girl," Greer says to Piper behind a cupped palm.

"That's never happened before," she replies from the corner of her mouth.

"I didn't even know he liked girls," Dylan chimes in, the entire commentary happening as if we weren't standing in front of them, within earshot.

"Same," Cameron adds. "I thought maybe he wasn't attracted to anyone, what's it called? Asexual."

That's too bad. Miller's husband was previously my favorite.

Bea shifts her weight onto one leg. "Definitely not." The confident announcement startles them speechless once more. "Heyyyy," she singsongs with a wave. "We can hear you."

She deserves better than my silence. I *ahem*, intentionally slowing my words to avoid a stammer, which would surely lead to more teasing. "This...is Behraz." Her name alone quiets the anxiety and I breathe in, gathering more confidence. "My girlfriend."

She flashes a glorious smile at the simple introduction and gives another wave, this one giddy and childlike. "Hi!"

I name them in age order and couples: Piper and Dylan, Greer and Lucas, then Cameron. They exchange stiff handshakes, still stupefied.

"What's that?" Piper tugs at my sleeve, eyeing the ink peeking out over my wrist. "You got a tattoo?"

"No way!" Greer pushes her aside to inspect it herself. "He's not cool enough for a tattoo."

I pull up the sweater sleeve to let them have a better look. "Bea drew it."

"That's nuts."

Is there no end to their slack-jawed responses? What happened to small talk and tokens of appreciation?

"Miller's not here?" Behraz looks to me for an answer.

Cam throws a mindless thumb past his shoulder. "She's in the basement with Park and the kids. I'll go call them up." He backpedals and disappears through a lit doorway.

Cautious footsteps come down the stairs one by one, faded orange curls bouncing on her shoulders. "Fletcher? Is that you?"

Bea loosens her grasp, but I don't let her. I climb two steps to meet her, keeping my girlfriend at my side.

"Hey, Mom."

She opens her arms and tucks into my shoulder, using one hand to bring my cheek down a few inches so she can reach it for a kiss. "Hi, sweet boy." The greeting is as warm and familiar as the embrace. Mom pats my cheek twice before releasing me. "How are you?"

"Good," I confirm, sharing a small smile. "Really good."

"I can see that." Her attention moves to Behraz, gaze sweeping over her excitedly.

"Can't be doing that good," Parker's voice cuts through. He approaches from the rear of the house, arms crossing when he gets to the back of the group. "Not with that shitty contract."

"Oh, *Parker*. Have some manners." My mother grimaces, dismissing him with a wave. "Not everything is about hockey."

His eyes roll to one side, averting them from Mom's glare. Her expression softens when her focus returns to Bea. "Introduce her to me, Fletcher."

"She's," I begin shyly, "Behraz."

"Hi, Beh-raz." The careful enunciation emphasizes the *h*. "Did I say it right?"

"Yeah-yes." Bea nods. "Hi...Fletcher's Mom." She immediately backpedals. "I mean, *uh*, Mrs. Donovan?"

"Please." Mom chokes on a laugh. "It's Riona. Seems like both of my sons have poor manners."

My loyal companion, the raging blush, worsens. "Sorry, this is my mom."

"I didn't realize," Bea replies dryly, then addresses my mom. "I'm the girlfriend."

Stifled laughter from the group has my blush worsening.

"I like you already." Mom wags a finger at her. "Fletch needs to have more fun people around him."

"*More* fun?" Piper chuckles, throwing up her arms. "He plays games for a living. His whole life is fun!"

"Lucky bastard," Dylan finally speaks up. "The rest of us are rotting in Summerside like overgrown Chanterelles." Laughter and high-fives are exchanged between my brothers-in-law as their wives chide them.

There's a crash, followed by a crunch from the basement. The adults erupt in a roar, arguing over whose kids it must have been, who started it, and who rightfully ended it.

"Go say hi to your dad," Mom yells to me over the commotion. The stampede goes to the basement, taking an unwilling Parker with them. "He's resting, but he's awake."

Of course, he's awake. Who could sleep in all this racket?

Our socked feet echo muted steps as we climb the stairs.

"Why do they call you Annie?"

My head sways in disappointment. "I have red hair."

The soft curve of her eyebrow rises, unconvinced. "You all have red hair."

"And I have the most freckles. Plus, I was an awkward, gangly kid. I spent most of my childhood reading in my bedroom and then fleeing to the fields to recreate dramatic scenes on my own." We turn at the landing.

Behraz shrugs. "I don't get it."

"They call me Anne of Green Gables, Bea. Ann with an e, Anne, Annie."

She rolls her eyes as we reach the top of the stairwell. "That's so..."

"...Lame?"

"Yes!" she says with a snap and a point, eyes brightening. "*Lame.* That's the word I was looking for." A scoff exits her lips with a sputter as we pad down the hallway. "It's not even an insult. Anne was freaking amazing." Lifting our clasped hands, she kisses my knuckles one by one. "But you're still Gilbert to me."

Wrinkles in my cheeks form from the contented grin stretching my face. It fades when I realize we're at my parents' bedroom door. I knock.

A grumble sounds from behind it.

"Dad?" The door creaks open. I peek through the sliver of light.

His sleeping form reclines against the headboard, supported by a few pillows, a generous beer belly covered by a summer blanket. The skin on his face and neck appears dull, speckled in red rashes, small lesions, and wrinkled like paper money. One large leg rests outside the sheets, the calf, ankle, and foot swollen and elevated on a triangle pil-low. A few lottery tickets are strewn next to his limp hand, sitting by a discarded pen.

"Dad?" I repeat.

He responds without moving. "*Hmm?*"

"It's Fletcher."

Both eyes open and widen, revealing a jaundiced hue instead of white around his honey-brown irises. My stomach lurches. The years of drin-king caught up to him. He's almost unrecognizable and more unwell than Miller described.

"Hey, kid." Dad weakly lifts his hand, and I cover it with mine, keeping it against the mattress. "You taking care of yourself?"

Bea tries to let go of me, but I don't allow it. I need her.

"Yeah." A long breath exits from my nose as I join him on the bed, half-sitting at the edge. "How about you?"

A sarcastic chuckle sounds from his throat. "Never been good at taking care of anyone, not even myself." Regret clouds his expression. "Wish I woulda learned how to earlier. Then I wouldn't feel like such a useless piece of shit for having to depend on everyone else now."

His rue reflects in mine. "You...took care of us. You worked—"

"No need to lie for my sake," he interrupts himself to cough a few ti-mes into his elbow. "I was barely around. Your mom," he coughs once more, "She did the heavy lifting with you kids. Piper and Park, too."

"It was enough."

"At the time," he sighs, "it felt like it was, but looking back..." Dad frowns, shaking his head in disagreement. His gaze drags to Bea at a snail's pace. "Is there someone with you, or am I seeing things?"

I push out a short laugh and look to her, who half-smiles at the floor. "Yeah, there is."

"Hiya." He waves a flaccid hand over his torso. "Sorry about meeting you in this state."

"Hi," she replies. "It's a pleasure."

"Fletch?" He beckons me closer with his hand. "You gonna tell me your girlfriend's name, or what?"

"Oh." I cringe at myself. "It's Behraz."

"Behraz? Pretty name."

"Thank you." Bea accepts the compliment, the apples of her cheeks turning pink.

"Come home more often, Fletcher." Dad turns his hand underneath mine, leaving it with a tight squeeze. "I'll be here all the time now."

"I will." It's a promise I don't know I can keep, but it's worth making to see his face brighten for a moment. Sudden clamor from downstairs has my father rubbing his temples with one hand. "Take it easy. We'll come check on you in a bit."

He nods and covers his eyes with the same hand. We tiptoe out, closing the door as quietly as possible.

Bea huffs air out through puffed cheeks, then curls an arm around my waist. "You okay, Fletcher?"

My arm wraps around her, too, needing her close. "I'm always okay when you're around. You make everything better."

That sweet beauty spot on her cheek dances when she smiles, and I peck her forehead.

She tips her head back to look at me, tempting me into another kiss. I give it to her, relishing the privacy, the warmth of her chest pressed into mine, our joined lips.

"*Ewwww*, Uncle Fletcher!"

I pull my lips into my mouth, face heating up with embarrassment. The oldest of my nephews stands akimbo on the top stair, sticking his tongue out. Typical eight-year-old shit. "Hey, Charlie."

"Not you, too! Mom and Dad are gross enough."

Bea hides her face in my chest. My heart skips, excited by her proximity. I'm tempted to tell him we're grown-ups and she's my girlfriend, so we'll do whatever the hell we want, but I decide to be the adult. "Is there something you need, bud?"

"Aunt Millie said not to bother you." He looks between us, ears reddening. "Said you had a special guest, but..."

"That's okay. What's going on?"

"*Um*." He nervously plays with the hem of his shirt. "Will you be 'it'? None of the other adults want to."

"*Hmm*." I tap a finger against my lips, faking disinterest. "Should I?"

Usually, I would have said yes right away, but I don't want to leave Bea alone with the rest of the family. Before I can agree, my girlfriend's head pops up. "If you don't want to, I will!"

"You will?" Charlie and I say together. His eyes go round.

Bea mirrors his wide smile and glimmers with excitement. "Sure! I haven't played tag in forever. Sounds like fun."

"Okay, c'mon then!" He trots down the steps, beckoning us with quick swoops of his arm. She escapes from me, squealing, and follows him with a gallop. "What's your name?"

"It's Bea."

Her voice sounds distant already, and I clamber down the staircase after them, grabbing my sneakers from the front before going to the backyard.

The whole gang's here: Charlie's sisters, Greer's two boys, even Miller's toddler stepdaughter, Raven.

My vision goes dark with the tied cloth, but the kids give themselves away. I capture two of them mercilessly, scooping each up in an arm. I let one down, then lift the blindfold, realizing I caught Charlie and Greer's youngest, Logan. Complaining groans reply.

"*No fair!*"

"*You cheated!*"

"Yeah, you're way bigger!" Logan protests, squirming from my hold.

"That's not what 'cheating' means."

"It's definitely not a fair match-up," Bea says, taking off her socks before walking onto the grass. She cracks her knuckles with a look of mischief, poking her tongue from the corner of her smiling mouth. "Is it my turn yet?"

Before I can warn them to take it easy, they've already blindfolded her with a rolled-up bandana. They all shriek and scatter as she spins, arms outstretched, staggering barefoot across the lawn. She almost trips over her feet a couple of times but manages to maintain balance.

"If you get tagged, you get tickled." She wiggles her fingers in the air, bellowing out a villainous laugh. My nieces and nephews giggle and scream, zigzagging around each other as Bea chases them like a short, busty Frankenstein.

What a goof.

God, I'm so fucking in love with her.

My sisters are in tears. Dylan and Lucas snort up their beers and use napkins to wipe away the dripping liquid from their faces. I think I see Parker let out a half-smile, but it disappears soon after. Mom covers her mouth to hide a laugh, but elbows me in the side as I approach. "She's wonderful, Fletch. Where the hell'd you find her?"

More like she found me.

"And she's stunning."

"Isn't she?" Pride bursts in my chest.

And she's mine.

"I've never seen you in love before," she says. "Except maybe that time you saw that blonde girl—*what's her name?*—in *The Mask*."

My eyes fall shut, a blush creeping up my neck.

"Oh, my God, you're so right, Mom!" Greer interrupts, slapping a hand to my shoulder. "You totally had a baby boner for Cameron Diaz!"

"Shut up."

"Hey, Pipe!" she calls. "Remember when Fletch wanted to watch *The Mask*, like, five times on Boxing Day?"

"Please, shut up."

"Watch?" Piper rolls her eyes and jerks her fist in the air. "I think we all know what he was doing."

Mom grumbles. "Piper, cut it out. That's disgusting."

"What he was doing was *definitely* disgusting."

I try to ignore the teasing and refocus on the game of tag. Behraz faces the back wall of the fence, hands moving over the painted wood, clearly lost. "*Ohhh*, I've caught someone," she sings.

Raven wraps around her leg and pulls. "That is not a real people! That a fence!"

Miller facepalms.

"Aha!" Bea tags the three-year-old's arm lightly. "Gotcha!" She slides the bandana from her eyes. Raven beams back, still latched on. "Did you want to get caught?"

My little niece replies with a series of nods.

"How *sneaky*."

"That's not how it works!" Piper's eldest, Lila, puts her hands on her hips and rolls her eyes. "Babies, man."

Piper hooks an arm around her daughter's neck. "Alright, kiddo, you can discuss the injustice of it all after getting washed up. Dinner's not gonna eat itself."

The evening air chills with the setting sun, a pink afterglow brightening the sky. Bea twirls the looped bandana around a finger. "Should I save this for later?"

"*Shhh*," I say through a laugh, leading her inside. "I've gotten enough shit from my sisters already. They don't need any more ammunition."

We settle around the table and get slices of turkey handed to us, passing the other parts of the meal back and forth: a salad, mashed potatoes and gravy, green beans, candied yams. I serve myself some cranberry sauce.

"It's the only thing I made at home." Mom points to the bowl with a fork. She's not a great cook as is, and there are too many people who don't want to cook instead, so for the past few years, we all chip in and get Thanksgiving dinner catered. "Your friend sent the cranberries in there from his family's farm. What's his name, again?"

"Oh, Landon?" Bea answers.

"Yep, that's the one."

Behraz nods. "The farm is out in the middle of nowhere Ontario, but it's gorgeous."

"You've been there?" Mom adds some more salad to Dad's plate, much to his chagrin.

"Oh, yeah. They invited me out there for the holidays when I couldn't visit my folks. Landon's married to Indi, my ex-boss who's now my best friend." She chews on a bite of salad. "We worked at the same law firm in Ottawa."

"*Ahh*, so you're a lawyer?" Greer pries. "We've all been wondering—"

"Yeah." A proud smile appears on her face. "I'm a lawyer."

My nephews and nieces get louder and louder. Miller hushes them from the kids' table and throws her voice. "What kind of lawyer are you, Behraz?"

"The firm specializes in libel and slander cases for high-profile clients," she explains, "but it's not what I'm interested in or articled for. And you can call me Bea." A silent swallow of wine splits the statement. "Everyone does."

"She's being humble." My hand slides to hers under the table, grasping and lacing our fingers together. "Bea has an apprenticeship starting in January with a prestigious firm in London."

Piper gasps while taking a sip from her glass, and I can't tell whether she's being facetious or sincere. "Fancy! What would you do there?"

"Mostly learning more about international law, reviewing past rulings, collecting evidence, observing court, stuff like that."

"*Ooh*, would you be working with war criminals like Amal Clooney?" Greer asks. The uneasy pit in my stomach isn't budging. I don't know if they're actually interested or if they're gonna somehow tear her apart like a bunch of vultures.

"Maybe! If anything, I'd be aiding in prosecuting them. Hopefully, we can take down a corrupt government official or two."

Dad complains of a stomachache, and my parents excuse themselves from the table, slowly scuffling toward the stairwell.

"Let me get this straight," Lucas adds through a chew. "You're friends with Radek's wife—"

"Yep. Gabe Finch, too."

The men at the table choke and sputter, cursing out their surprise. "The one on CSN?"

"Yeah." Bea shrugs. "She and Indi were roommates at uni."

"Damn."

"Holy shit."

Cameron pipes up. "She and Fletch's goalie recently got married, right? I think I saw the announcement on CSN."

Bea hums in confirmation. "They did, yeah."

"*Got it*. That must be how you met." Greer nods in understanding. "Through the WAGs of the Regents."

There it is. I don't appreciate the insinuation and send a glare her way.

"You'd think." Bea's tone is unfazed. "But we never really got the chance to until I ran into him while riding my bike."

Parker hasn't said a word the entire meal, but he puts his fork down. "Ran into?"

"It's an expression, Park," Piper replies. "She didn't *actually* run into him."

Behraz laughs, but it's usual ability to dissolve my anxiety is countered by my family's ability to stir it up. "No, I actually *did* run into him. Direct hit."

The adult side chatter goes quiet.

"It's kinda funny if you think about it," she continues through a titter. "Poor man was minding his own business, crossing the street, and I knocked him out. Flat," —her fork stabs a small shred of turkey— "Horizontal" —another stab at another piece— "Man was out cold."

My older brother blinks twice. A muscle in his jaw tics.

Uh oh.

His eyes narrow, focus switching between her and me. "*You*...knocked him out?"

"Totally," she says through a giggle. The rate of my pulse accelerates. "I may be short, but I'm strong."

Parker's eyes fix squarely on me. "Did she give you a concussion?"

She notices my lack of response and slows her bites. Any trace of joy in her eyes fade into apology, voice suddenly mousy. "It was an accident."

My hand meets her thigh, squeezing the flesh in comfort and confirmation. She did nothing wrong. If anything, it's my fault for not telling them.

Parker scoffs, his contempt palpable. "An accident that affects his profession."

"*Pfft*." Dylan blows a raspberry, attempting to deflect the sudden tension. "Head injuries happen all the time in the NHL. He seems fine."

Cameron adds fuel to the fire. "Exactly. It coulda been so much worse."

"True." My brother glowers and huffs. "She coulda caused permanent damage and he'd never play again."

Something inside me snaps.

"Shut up, Park." It comes out softer than I want.

"Not that he cares about that or anything." His loathing transfers to me. "Didn't care to call his own family."

My face gets three degrees hotter, repeating the command louder, more firmly. "I said, shut up."

"C'mon guys." Greer tries to dissipate the brewing confrontation. "It's been months since we've seen each other. Can't we have one peaceful meal together?"

"Sure." Parker drops his napkin onto his plate, scraping the legs of the chair across the floor before standing. "Enjoy your *peaceful meal*."

Bea goes ashen. For a moment, I weigh my options, wondering if it's a good idea to leave her with my sisters and go after Parker, but anger diminishes any logic. It crawls over every inch of my reddened skin. I jump to my feet.

"Fletch—" Piper and Greer say simultaneously.

"Don't," I cut them off, gritting through my teeth, "I've had enough."

Following the sound of his heavy footsteps leads to the rec room. My asshole brother rounds the foosball table, grabs a beer from the mini fridge, and opens it with a loud *pop*.

"Hey!"

He slouches into the couch, takes a long gulp, then belches. "Oh, *now* you wanna talk."

"Shut the fuck up and listen to me, for *once*." Cursing at my brother feels unfamiliar on my tongue and takes a second to get used to. "I'm so sick of your bullshit. You wanna be a dick to me, fine, be my fucking guest." My arms move around mid-air. "I'm used to it. But that's *my* girlfriend. You won't be disrespecting her again, got it? She's the only reason I'm here."

He scoffs. "Yeah? Dad slowly dying or spending time with your *actual* family wasn't convincing enough?"

"Fuck you." My index finger points, direct and accusing, emboldened by simmering rage. "Don't act like you're some sort of saint because you live on the next block and cut their grass every week. You're not the only one pulling weight—"

He takes another glug of beer. "Yeah, throwing all that money around solved everyone's problems, eh?"

I growl, frustrated. "It always comes down to money with you, doesn't it? You don't give a fuck that I got hurt, but if I couldn't play, you'd have to actually do shit like take care of Mom and Dad."

"Okay, Fletch, sure. Keep telling yourself that *I'm* the bad guy. You think your little girlfriend out there doesn't care about money? You think Bea's with you for what, your athletic prowess and brilliant mind?"

Yeah, asshole. And my huge dick.

"Get fucked, Parker." The large coffee table bars the space between us. Probably for the best, otherwise I'd reach over and punch her name right out of his mouth. Then I'd be no better than him. "You don't know shit about her. She may have hit me, but at least she was sorry about it."

That one seems to sting. His eyes darken over the top of the can. "Me checking you on the ice is the reason you could take it."

"I was a kid." Hurt smolders in my chest, as if it happened last week instead of fifteen years ago.

"And now you're a man. All grown-up and keeping secrets, making reckless decisions that affect all of us."

"Reckless for who, exactly? Yeah, it was pretty reckless not to tell you

I had a severe concussion. Reckless to allow a near-stranger to care for me over my own family. Now, why would I do that, huh, Park? You forget already?" Steam has to be coming out of my ears by now with how vehemently I'm sweating from this verbal diarrhea. "*You* told me not to come home, because *you* think I'm not good enough, not capable of making the right choice—no, the choice that *you* want me to make. *You* think, *you* want. And that's what goes. Nothing anybody else thinks, wants, or says matters. Right? You know what's best for *everyone*." The word exaggerates with my jazz hands and a singing lilt.

"And what about you?" Parker rolls his eyes and shakes his head, denying and disapproving in the simple motion. "You used to be so focused, locked in. Now you don't give a damn about hockey, too busy with playing house and fucking around with—" A dismissive hand flails in the air, motioning toward the door.

"What did I say about disrespecting my girlfriend, Park?" I warn, a finality stabilizing my tone. One set of knuckles cracks under the pressure of my other hand. "Say one more thing about her."

Parker's eyebrows rise and drop while lifting a palm in surrender.

The breaths taken through my nostrils steady from harsh intakes of air. "She's the best thing to ever happen to me."

A humorless laugh leaves his chest. "The best thing?"

"Yeah, the *best* thing." I lower to the opposing armchair with a sigh, and scrub my face, wholly tired of the argument. "You don't get to tell me how to fucking feel about the woman I love." He nurses his drink, possibly accepting he's not gonna win this time. "You think I wanna be in here, fighting with you? That I wouldn't rather be enjoying the rare free time I have with the people I love?"

My brother doesn't say anything, simply sips his drink and fidgets with the pop tab while I continue. "I'm sorry you didn't get to have the career you dreamed of, Parker. It sucks." His eyes go glassy at the mention. "And I know you don't think so, but I *am* grateful for everything you did for me. I just...can't keep living for you. I'm not a vessel you can fill with your expectations and shit in whenever I don't live up to them. I'm a person, Park."

Our eyes lock, but the hardened outer layer has melted from them. "And you're my big brother. I want you to be happy, I wanna make Mom and Dad happy. But I wanna be happy, too. Hockey isn't my dream, it's yours."

The conversation stills for a beat. Parker stares at the rug between his socked feet. "So what, you're gonna quit?"

"I didn't say that. Hockey is my job. I enjoy it sometimes, too, and I'm gonna keep playing, but not for you. Now, Behraz? *She's* my dream, and I'll do anything to keep her. One day, that might mean quitting hockey."

It's the worst thing I could threaten him with.

"But not today," I end. This is probably the longest conversation I've had with him, ever. "She'd never ask that of me, anyway."

Another pause hangs in the air, thick with the uncertainty of how Park will react.

He clears his throat. "Fletcher."

For a second, he throws me a sorry glance, and my heart pangs with guilt. But it passes as quickly as it came.

"You don't owe me anything, Parker." I straighten, getting to my feet and casting a tall shadow over him. "I don't expect or need an apology from you. But when you come back in there, you're going to tell Bea you're sorry for being a jerk."

My nervous system is wrecked. I've never spoken to anyone like that, much less my brother. I duck into the washroom in the hall on my way back to the dining table. Splashing cold water on my face helps enough to encourage a return to the chaos.

Miller and Cam have since switched spots, and all the women in my family, save Harper, have their elbows on the tabletop, leaning toward Behraz. My sisters stare at me with knowing, almost sinister, smiles. I slide into my seat next to Bea. She locks her hand onto mine under the table.

"You okay, Annie?" Piper grins.

My girlfriend pushes her plump lips forward, and wrinkles her nose, unable to hide her distaste for the nickname. "I really don't think it's cool to call him that unless he asks you to."

Her grin drops, eyes shifting to me.

"I've never really been a fan," I admit.

Greer coughs when Parker sneaks back into the dining room. "Anyway, we were just talking about how we had no idea you two were living together."

Oh, great.

Parker closes his eyes and sighs through his nostrils.

Behraz titters. "That's a funny story, too."

"You're full of funny stories, huh?" Piper sneers.

I glare back at her, mouthing the words *be nice*.

Bea either doesn't notice the snark or doesn't care. Her sweet face remains unbothered, smiling into her next bite. "You have no idea. For every instance Fletcher is quiet and restrained, I am overly chatty and delightfully clumsy. Hence, bicycle accident."

A chorus of understanding or agreement replies.

We tag-team the explanation of how she stuck around to aid in my recovery, how I found out her sublease had ended and offered a temporary place to stay, and how living together, as friends at first, only deepened our mutual admiration.

Not as poetically as that, but you know. "And the rest is history" is a surefire way to end an interrogation.

"Well, I think it's sweet, Fletch," Mom says, handing out dessert plates of pumpkin pie. "Your first love being your one and only is really special."

Greer makes a lewd motion, forming a V with her fingers and flicking her tongue through it when Mom turns her back. Bea's eyes widen with an instant flush, and I use my middle finger to wipe my tear duct.

"Grow up," Miller grumbles.

Parker pounds the back of his fork onto the table, clearly annoyed at how all the siblings return to our pubescent dynamics when we're together too long. "That's enough." Everyone's attention turns to him. "Hey, *um*, Bea? I'm sorry." The clatter of metal on porcelain ceases. Greer's bite falls out of her open mouth back onto her plate. "For the way I acted earlier. I was upset with Fletcher and rude to you."

She accepts with a nod, throwing me a fleeting, surprised look. *Wow*, she mouths.

My sisters chime in altogether.

"Sorry."

"Yeah, we're really sorry."

One hand smooths over Bea's back.

"I get it," my girlfriend replies. "I have an overprotective brother, too. I just happen to be outrageously in love with yours. I promise I have the best of intentions."

Greer opens her mouth, surely to say something inappropriate, and I stop her.

"By the way, we're staying at a hotel for this weekend before I head out to Calgary."

If flabbergasted had a sound, this was it.

"Well!" Mom claps her hands together, silencing the protest. "Who's ready for pie?"

The pumpkin and cherry pies get cleaned out before we can fight over the last slices, and when the kids revolt about going to bed, their respective sets of parents take them upstairs, leaving Bea and I to clear the table while my mother packs the leftovers in the kitchen.

"I heard what you said," she murmurs.

My eyebrow perks.

"I know I shouldn't have eavesdropped, but I was worried. I don't think anyone's stood up for me like that."

"I surprised myself. I've never even stood up to him, either."

"I'm so proud of you." She leaves her stack of plates onto the one in my hand, strokes up my flexed forearm with a hum, and uses my shoulders to lift herself to the tips of her toes, pulling my face toward her to place a kiss on my cheek. A blush rises to meet her lips in a hot wave. Bea releases a breathy sigh by my ear, and my cock stirs. The bastard.

"When you blush like this...*God*, Fletcher. It makes me so wet."

I swallow.

"Can't wait to get to the hotel so I can suck your perfect cock."

"Shit." I discard the plates on the table and grasp her hand, pulling her toward the kitchen. "I have an idea."

My mom's inattention allows us to sneak past her and into the renovated, walk-in pantry.

"In here?" Bea gapes, backing herself into some wooden shelves. "You're turning out to be such a slut."

I pin her on the spot, stretching her hands to the high shelf above her head. She arches, pushing her tits toward me. A gritty groan climbs the column of my neck. "You drive me crazy, you know that?" My lips drop to graze her jaw before gripping her thighs and sliding her up, hooking both knees over my hips. "I'm so hard I could cry, Bea."

One harsh, denim-covered thrust creates an intolerable friction. The glass jars rattle behind us.

"Dying to be inside you. Dying to see how wet you are." Her bottom lip mutes a whimper when I squeeze one breast, thumbing over a hardened nipple. "You'll be quiet for me, won't you?"

She shakes her head. "Let 'em hear, Fletcher. I want them to know how well-fucked you keep me."

CHAPTER 28:
CLIMB INTO MY SKIN AND STAY THERE

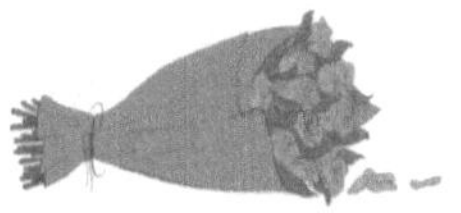

BEHRAZ

March

TIME WITH FLETCHER NEVER FEELS LIKE ENOUGH.

The two-month trial of only seeing him between series of road games didn't prepare me for the long stretches apart. It was tolerable for the first couple of weeks of the new year. Post-winter holiday festivities continued, and this island on the other side of the Atlantic Ocean felt cheery. But the beginning of spring is wet and cold and lonely and depressing.

It's no help that the radiator in this apartment swings between freezing to so hot I can't breathe. Or that there's a sticky note on my fridge in Fletcher's handwriting that says, "No hot girl dinners while I'm gone!" serving as a constant reminder that my boyfriend knows me too well and it's exactly what I'd be doing if not for the stern warning.

And it's only March. I mean, phone sex is hot and all, and I know I'm being a needy, whiny, spoiled human, but it's not the same thing. Logically, my brain says it doesn't matter if I'm in Ottawa or London if he's gone all the time, but being *this* far from him for *this* long? It's becoming unbearable. Which makes this next conversation that much more painful.

My thumb hovers over the word Dreamboat on my phone screen, yearning to hear the calm, deep timbre of his voice. I accidentally hit the message icon, and the view changes to our most recent exchanges.

ME

Did you know you make my heart race??

DREAMBOAT

Did you know you make my heart beat?

ME

Swooooon. You always say the best things.

DREAMBOAT

That's because you are the best thing

ME

God, I miss you. I wanna kiss you. Like right now.

DREAMBOAT

You were the first

ME

And I'll be your last!!

DREAMBOAT

Damn right. And everything in between.

ME

blowing kiss emoji I love you so goddamn much.

A long sigh exits my nose. I squint one eye while studying the clock, wondering what time it is in Seattle and if he made it back to the hotel after his game or if they flew back right after, but the mental gymnastics require too many brain cells and I've only got the one on this particular night. I shoot my shot and hope for the best.

ME

Is now a good time to talk?

DREAMBOAT

Gimme 2 mins

ME

Okayyyyy

The intercom for the outside door of my apartment building buzzes, and I hit the button to allow entry. I shouldn't be ordering food so late, but the caseload has been grueling, and I skipped dinner entirely. Fish and chips are no replacement for poutine, but some semblance of French fries is better than nothing. In my rush to answer the series of heavy knocks, I trip over my own feet, face-first into the wooden door. It temporarily stuns me, but I manage to twist the knob open, sucking air through my teeth while rubbing a palm over the sore spot. My squint widens, returning my vision.

A tall redhead greets me, brown bag in hand, his serene smile splitting the constellations of freckles on his face. My heart thumps wildly at his starry-eyed gaze and the way he adjusts the travel duffle slung over the shoulder of his Regents-branded black puffer.

Snap out of it, Behraz.

It's ridiculous. I miss that man so much, I'm hallucinating. Poor delivery guy must think I'm nuts. I blink three times, but it still looks like Fletcher.

"You okay, gorgeous?"

I gape. "Sorry?"

His smile widens, lifting a bright red blush up his cheeks. "Were you expecting someone else?" He shakes the paper bag. "Other than the guy who dropped this off."

I break. Tears that didn't exist a second ago pour from me in messy streaks. From exhaustion of the many long days and late nights without him to help finish crosswords or remind me to drink water or to assure me that yes, taking breaks is necessary and deserved.

"Aw, baby." Fletcher scoops me up with one arm around my waist, and my legs hook around him. His quieting shushes and gentle kisses elicit ugly sniveling from me as he pushes through the entryway. I cling to him like an awkward spider monkey.

"How...are you here?"

"I missed you," he explains, lowering to the vintage, rust-colored settee that came with the place. The small loveseat barely contains us, at least until the duffle strap slides down his arm and onto the floor. Fletcher kisses the ridges of my knuckles sitting on both of his shoulders. "Had two days between games and I'd rather be with you than alone in Ottawa."

"What about—"

He answers the question before I can get it out. "I'll fly back in time to play Chicago on Saturday."

"It's too much." My arms circle his neck, fingers burying into the lush auburn mess on his head while I pelt kisses all over that sweet, handsome face.

"It's not. I love you." Fletcher peers down at me through those thick lashes as if I hung every last star in the light-polluted London sky by hand. "And there's no way I was gonna miss your birthday."

It's the seventh? D'oh! Only I'd be so scatter-brained as to forget my own birthday.

"I love you. And I missed *you*," I gush. "Missed how your skin tastes slightly salty from sweat." My lips brush against his grown-out facial hair. "How your beard tickles." My palms coast across the strong sinews of his forearms. "How you hold me."

"Can I kiss you now, too?" Fletcher smooths a thumb over my chin before sweeping away the messy ends of my ponytail from my shoulder and cradling my jaw.

I hum and nod.

"Thank fuck." He draws our lips together, slipping his tongue inside my mouth, intentional and savoring, only stopping to drop his head into the crook of my neck, pulling himself into me and me into him until we can't possibly be any closer, as if he wants to climb into my skin and stay there. To be honest, I'd let him.

Three hours later, Fletcher snoozes against my belly, drawn-out breaths fanning across the bare skin. I'm lulled by the delicious weight of his naked chest across my lower torso and hips, stresses of casework all but faded. Until I remember.

"Fletcher?" I whisper, toying with the swoops of deep red waves crowning his head. "You awake?"

He confirms with a pleasured noise.

A knot of unease tightens within me, beneath the spot his head rests. "I got offered a clerkship at the ICJ."

"That's 'cause you're incredible," Fletcher mumbles. "I'm so proud of you."

The laugh I use to accept the compliment is dry, humorless, and I get the sense he didn't quite process what it means. "It's at The Hague. I'd have to live in the Netherlands for ten months."

His eyes flash open, sable hues suddenly bright and alert. "What?"

My mouth tugs downward. "I'm sorry."

"For what?" Fletcher lifts from me for a moment, then pushes an arm behind my back to roll us to our sides, crushing our fronts together.

"For wanting a career that's keeping us apart."

"Don't." He kisses my clammy forehead, then the tip of my nose. "You've worked so hard." He kisses the frown, too, melting it away. "When would it start?"

"June."

"Perfect."

I titter from disbelief. "Perfect? How is it perfect?"

"My contract extension is up by then." The man grins, downright giddy. "We can find a place together."

Disbelief persists with an incessant shaking of my head. "Wait, wait, wait...let me get this straight."

Fletcher giggles.

"You'll walk away from a team and city you love, to...be with...*me*?"

"Bea," he starts, tone shifting to something more serious. "I'd do anything for you."

"But what about *your* career?"

"I'll figure it out," he says with a shrug. "Europe has hockey leagues, too, y'know. My agent's been asking about what's next and trying to get things lined up. Now I can give him a legit answer."

"But—" The protest is worthless.

"Do you not want me here?"

"Of course, I want you here. Just not at the expense of—"

"Ah, ah, ah." His long first finger presses to my parted mouth and silences my argument. "Nothing is gonna be at the expense of anything. And even if it is," Fletcher adds, "it'll be worth a lifetime of happiness with you."

My eyes narrow, brimming with fresh tears. "If this was your attempt to make me cry, then I hate to tell you," —one fat, hot drop escapes— "it worked."

Fletcher wipes it away. "So, you'll have me?" His mouth teases, begging for another kiss.

I let him steal one, and one more for good measure. "Don't I already have you?"

"Touché." He releases me and scooches down, going back to his original position on my stomach. "Promise me something?"

"Anything."

"I'll have to tell the team eventually. You'll be there, right?"

"Yeah," I agree. "You're never getting rid of me."

EPILOGUE

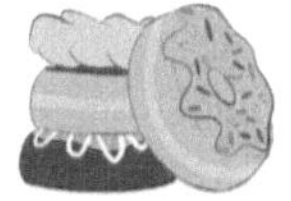

FLETCHER

Two Years Later

"DO YOU THINK THAT, MAYBE, IF YOU SQUEEZE MY hand, we'll land in time to only be a little late for Gabe's baby shower?"

Oh, Behraz. My sweet, optimistic sun ray. That ship sailed six hours ago when our flight from Frankfurt was delayed due to the masses traveling for the winter holidays.

An unsure sound grumbles from my chest. "I don't know, but worth a shot." I give our twined hands a good squeeze before plucking a kiss from where they connect.

"Or maybe we could talk to the pilot about our situation, and he'll fly faster?" Bea rattles off. "Oh! What if we show him that really cute video of the cats when they were kittens and tussling around like roly-polies? Maybe we can FaceTime the sitter, and he can watch their silliness live? You think he likes cats? I don't know, I'm throwing out any and all ideas."

"Hmmm," I wonder aloud, stifling a knowing grin. "Any chance you're nervous to get to Ottawa?"

She releases a groaning sigh. "How'd you know?"

"I have a knack for it. Special nerve-detection powers." I wrinkle my nose, teasing. "But why's that?" My thumb rubs the spot at the base of her left hand's ring finger, like I've done since she first let me hold her hand. But this time, the space is occupied with dark blue sapphires circling the Nishapur turquoise set on a rose gold band.

"Oh, no reason in particular!" Bea throws her free arm up in exasperation within our business class suite. "It's not like we secretly eloped in Spain this summer or anything."

My grin goes devilish. "We did do that, didn't we?"

It was perfect. Simple, private. So many of my dreams came true within the span of just a few hours.

Behraz fakes a whiny sob. "What if they get mad? Indi and Gabe are scary older sister-types. I'm a younger sister. I'm not built for that kinda scrutiny—"

"Hey, listen," I cut in. "They won't be anything but happy for us."

The worry line splitting her brow persists. "Yeah?"

I nod. "Especially after they see the pictures."

The afterglow of the setting sun from the top of El Tajo De Ronda in Málaga bathed Bea in soft light, making everything a deeper shade than it already was: her flower crown of bougainvillea and pale pink hibiscus, her salmon-colored gown, the shade of her lips. The stone arches of the bridge over the gorge, the surging waterfall below; it was nothing short of a fairy tale, a fantasy world coming to life from beyond the pages of my imagination.

"You're right," my wife concedes. "But just this once."

I lose myself in the stunning memory, cherishing the best day of my life for a few moments until she interrupts.

"We're not gonna make it to Gabe's baby shower, are we?"

"Sorry, my love." I tut. "Looks like the hand squeezing didn't work."

Her head hangs in disappointment, and I take the opportunity to leave a kiss on her hair. "We'll head over first thing tomorrow, after a decent night's rest at home."

"Okay."

Visits to Ottawa had been few since we moved abroad, alternating holidays between Prince Edward Island and meeting her family in Dubai, but we kept the apartment. I couldn't get myself to sell the place where we first fell in love. Everything else could be temporary, but this way, it'd always be ours.

"I have an idea." My elbow nudges her arm. "Might not work, but maybe it'll make you feel better."

Her gaze slides to mine, open to yet wary of the suggestion. She continues to pout. It doesn't make her lips any less tempting.

"What if I kiss you until you can't stop smiling?"

The plush pink bow of her mouth turns up at the edges. "That might be nice. Will there be tongue?"

"If you want."

"Oh, good." Her mouth closes into mine as we lean towards each other. "I've been meaning to cross 'make out with the love of my life on an airplane' off my bucket list."

"What a coincidence," I tease. "Me too."

———

The elevator up to Wade and Gabe's penthouse dings at every floor. I'd sent a message in the group chat when we landed, and a last-minute brunch got thrown together.

I've ridden this thing a hundred times, but it feels different today. I'm married. To Behraz Irani. A woman I fantasized about for most of my twenties.

"You're staring," Bea clips.

Am I not supposed to be? She's gorgeous, and right when I think I can't possibly love her any more, I surprise myself. It's nothing short of miraculous that I find myself loving her more every day.

"It's the dress, isn't it?" she asks, pulling her coat panels over her chest. "It's too tight."

I deny the ridiculous claim. "It's perfect."

Behraz rolls her eyes to me, not wanting to believe it.

"You're perfect."

"Well, if you don't quit looking, my nipples are gonna get hard and everyone will see."

"Worse things have happened." My head tips in her direction, close enough for my lips to skim the shell of her ear. "What if I want everyone to, huh? What if I want them to know how worked up I can get my wife without touching her?"

She glares. "You're really horny in the morning."

My confidence soars, and it's all because of her. "Learned from the best."

"I've created a monster."

The doors split open, and Wade and Gabe await us in the open doorway of their unit, welcoming us in with bright expressions.

"Donny!"

"Not letting go of that nickname, huh?"

Gabe and Bea coo over her growing belly while I slap Wade lightly across the face. He returns the favor before we break into laughter and pull each other into a tight embrace. Their joy is infectious.

I jab his arm. "Look at ya. Baby Boner's all grown up."

"That's Daddy, to you," Wade gloats.

"*Ew*," Gabe intones. "He is *not* calling you that."

"Seconded." Bea shakes her head. "The only person he'll call Daddy is *me*."

"That doesn't even make sense." Wade waves it off, but looks to me and stops. "But then again, it kinda does."

The door swings open, and Landon and Indi stride in, each carrying a child wearing matching grey puffers. We repeat the exercise.

"Oh, hey, Captain." Landon offers a side hug while Akhila clutches his torso. "Swiss League looks good on you, bud."

"Lucked out." A hockey club happened to be recruiting to build a new team, and being a veteran player paid off. I motion to Bea, who's fawning over the girls. "I got a helluva lucky charm."

"I know how it goes." Landon slides his eyes to his wife. "I got one of those, too."

"They're getting so big, Indi," my wife coos.

Indi agrees but interrupts herself with a squeal. "What is that!" She grabs Bea's hand, drawing attention to the ring on her finger.

Landon gasps.

"What is that?" Behraz redirects, pointing to the swell of Indi's midsection. "Are you pregnant again?"

"Yep. Are you two married?"

There's nothing to be embarrassed about, and yet Bea and I both weather through a stormy blush. "Yes," she and I say together.

Pterodactyl screeches ending in congratulations from the four adults incite the two little girls into terrified wails. The group hug doled out doesn't help console them either.

Heavy barks join in the ruckus as scampering paws and a furry tail whips about to break up the huddle.

"Jesus." Jaeger tugs on Doug's leash and shushes the overexcited golden retriever. "Calm down, bud."

Wade gets down on one knee and babbles in baby talk while scrunching up Doug's face and playing with his ears. "You're such a good boy! Don't listen to that old grump. We're all so happy for Fletch, yes, we are..."

"*Aw*, man, what'd we miss?" Skylar whines.

"Indi's pregnant."

"Bea and Fletcher got married."

Skylar's eyes go wide at the simultaneously blurted statements. "I knew about the first part, but *whoa*. When did that happen?"

"Storytime?" I didn't expect anything less from Landon, the overeager gossip.

"Put it up on the TV so we can all see," Wade adds, walking over to the living area.

We gather on the sectional, throwing coats in a pile before going through the series of professional photographs and a short highlights video. Indi and Gabe flank my wife and grasp both of her hands.

"That's incredible." Wade gasps as the video zooms out, the shot capturing the entire bridge and the cliffside.

Landon *ooh*s. "They must've used one of those drones. So sick."

I catch our wives welling up. Indi kisses Behraz's temple. Gabe wipes their tears away.

"You three act so tough," Wade says through a chuckle, "you're such softies for each other."

Gabe warns him with a glare. "Don't make me hurt you."

"Don't threaten me with a good time." He reclines, elbows lifted, hands behind his back, manspreading his legs. It's the Wade I've always known. So much has changed, and so much has stayed the same.

"*Anyway*," Skylar singsongs. "Jaeg and I have news, too."

The screen connection switches to her phone, and they share pictures of the infant they're in the process of adopting.

We round robin, taking turns to show pictures and share stories of our lives that weren't passed around in the group chat. Akhila and Ellora swimming in the Atlantic Ocean. Our two cats, an orange tabby named Cheddar and a Russian blue called Luna dressed as Mario and Luigi during Halloween. Wade and Gabe at a charity basketball shootout.

Some families aren't blood. They're found, created, nurtured. And it's a calming feeling to return to this family: a growing, chosen group where there's no awkwardness or walking on eggshells as we pick up where we left off, just the warmth and support of my three brothers and sisters, despite the spans of time between our last in-person conversations.

Surrounded by the family I once upon a time only dreamed of, I realize I'm finally the main character I read about.

I turn my head to Bea. Her eyes glimmer with a soft smile and affirmation. The glance we exchange says everything. There's no joy I can't share, no obstacle I can't traverse.

How lucky am I to get to carry the love of the person I adore most in my heart and soul, and know she does the same?

And the fact that I get to do it alongside Landon and Indi, Wade and Gabe, and Jaeg and Skylar, each examples of great loves on their own, is icing on the cake.

Between us lies a whole world, a lifetime of love stories left to experience.

THE END

ACKNOWLEDGEMENTS

This book, y'all. This book nearly ended me. Like the rest of the characters in the Ottawa Regents, Fletcher and Behraz have been living in my head since 2021, and I was both excited to get to know them better and nervous to tell their story in the way I knew they deserved.

They're so different from the first two couples in the series. They're soft. They're losers (in their eyes.) They're trying to figure out where they belong in the world when it seems like everyone is moving on. They're every person in their late twenties, and many in their thirties and forties. Maybe even fifties, but I'm not there yet so I can't tell you for sure.

Fletcher and Behraz's happily-ever-after proved tough to put into words as so many things in our world crash and burn and life brought on hit after hit. However, like with nearly all challenges, the result was well worth it.

There are some very personal topics discussed throughout this book: Fletcher's social anxiety, Bea's late-diagnosis/adult ADHD and learning disability pull from my own experiences and loved ones affected by them. I'm not officially diagnosed, but there are signs. This is also for my brother, who has two post-graduate degrees despite a late-diagnosis (during medical school!) of ADHD and a word processing learning disability. Writing Bea felt like looking through his eyes with my own glasses and truly seeing him and myself in her.

I couldn't have gotten this book done without the incredibly supportive and encouraging community who advised me to pause, rest, then (respectfully) bullied me into writing.

There are countless times Cristina, Maria, Giuliana or Elle sent a message checking on me, how writing was going, or to scream with me about something my characters did or said. Beliz gave me the inside scoop on the hidden gems in Ottawa that Fletcher and Bea would love. Jess mostly sent pictures of her unfolded laundry on her bed at 10 p.m., but the same nonsense was happening at my house, so I felt less alone. Cassandra lent me her thoughts as a law student with ADHD. E talked trash during March

Madness and will pay for it at Sports Romance Con if it's the last thing I do. Millie made me laugh to the point of tears and tummy hurt on dark days and I can't thank her enough.

To Isabel for sprinting with me constantly to get this manuscript to the finish line while juggling all the things and still making time to remind me I'm okay. Can't wait to hug you so tight very soon! (For real, this time!)

Amelie, you're one of my first friends on this wild journey and I'm so honored that we get to do it together. Thank you for opening your heart and creative mind to me and allowing me to bounce ideas and vent and learn from you. I'll never be a whole ass aesthetic like you, but I'll die trying. You're getting a big hug soon, too!

To my alpha readers, Erin, Leigh, Reanne, Afreen, and Bekah who are so, so patient and kind through the super rough, early draft of this sweet story.

To my beta and sensitivity readers, Apoorva, Bee, Nik, Carla, Emily, Elizabeth, Carole, Faydia, Kim, Paro, and Zab. Your honest, invaluable feedback, genuine excitement, and gentle but constructive criticism improved this story tenfold.

To Lindsey Clarke, my forever editing angel. I've still not conquered em dashes. Commas are a mystery. Your patience is nothing short of saintly and despite my best efforts not to put you through the waiting-game wringer again, I fear I have let you down. You took it in stride, and I literally will not do this to you any more times. I mean it!

To the brilliant cover artists I've had the wonderful opportunity to collaborate with again, Allie Wygonik and Kell from Little Pluto Design: you've once more brought my characters to life and watching you grow in your craft is such a joy to witness. And I absolutely can't forget to thank Margherita, who put the work in to make the interior formatting clean and crisp.

To my desi girl author crew who inspire me everyday: Ava, Bal, NM, Esha, Vai, Anna P, Varsha, Riya, Khushi, Victoria, Ruby K, and Swati. I'm forever grateful for you all. Seeing more and more of us represent ourselves in the stories we write musters courage and hope.

To all the readers and authors I've connected with this past year and a half and beyond: thank you for seeing me and hearing my voice in a world where I'm often passed by and unheard, and made to feel undeserving and unworthy of being in this space.

And last, but in no way the least, to my husband who continuously sacrifices so much of our time together so I can chase my dreams. I'm sorry for the person I am when writing a book and preparing for release, haha. And in general. I'm insufferable. Thank you for being patient with your mentally unstable wife. Love you always, in this lifetime and the next.

All of you are responsible for getting this book up, so if it sucks, that's on you.

ABOUT THE AUTHOR

Ruby Rana is an elder millennial who writes spicy, funny and heartfelt romance about sassy brown girls. She excels in sending messages where autocorrect has gone terribly wrong.

When she's not battling typos, you can find her explaining Midwestern slang to her East Coast-raised husband, running after her young children or experimenting with new recipes in the kitchen.

Want to connect further? You can find her on the following platforms:

Instagram: rubyranawrites
Threads: rubyranawrites
TikTok: rubyranawrites
Goodreads: rubyranawrites
Amazon: Ruby Rana

Ruby Rana is also the author of Snap Shot (Ottawa Regents, Book 1), and Butterfly Effect (Ottawa Regents, Book 2).